PENGUIN BO

A HALF-BAKED LOVE STORY

Anurag Garg is an engineering graduate from BVCOE, New Delhi. Random thoughts, eligible to be put together in the form of a story, dragged him to his destiny, and he finally found his forte in writing. He finds himself close to nature and believes in creating circles of love and service around him. He lives in New Delhi and works in the IT industry.

Gunjan Narang, an aspiring educationist, was born in Delhi. She embraces reading and writing as her escape from the real world as well as a window to it. She wishes to explore the unexplored places of the world and write about the fast-evaporating everyday life of people.

Also by Anurag Garg

Love . . . Not for Sale!

ANURAG GARG

GUNJAN NARANG

PENGUIN BOOKS

PENGUIN BOOKS

USA | Canada | UK | Ireland | Australia
New Zealand | India | South Africa | China

Penguin Books is part of the Penguin Random House group of companies
whose addresses can be found at global.penguinrandomhouse.com

Published by Penguin Random House India Pvt. Ltd
7th Floor, Infinity Tower C, DLF Cyber City,
Gurgaon 122 002, Haryana, India

First published by Penguin Books India 2016

10 9 8 7 6 5 4 3 2

This is a work of fiction. Names, characters, places and incidents are either the product of the authors' imagination or are used fictitiously and any resemblance to any actual person, living or dead, events or locales is entirely coincidental.

ISBN 9780143426455

Typeset in Adobe Garamond Pro by Manipal Digital Systems, Manipal
Printed at Repro Knowledgecast Limited, India

www.penguin.co.in

The greatest pleasure in life is doing what people say you can't do.

To all those who motivated us!

Untying the Knot

'So, do you love me, Aarav?' Radhika asked, as she unzipped her blue denim shorts.

We were sitting inside my car in the minus fourth floor parking arena of Select Citywalk Mall in Saket. The car had tinted windows, so nothing was visible on the outside.

'What kind of a silly question is that? What has happened to you? I told you not to gulp down so many shots at one go!' I replied sternly as I stroked her sleek, long hair.

I was in the driver's seat with her on my lap. 'Oh, shut up, Aarav! I was just wondering if this is love or something else . . . because every time we meet, I feel like there's a spark missing in us . . . don't you . . .' I interrupted to pacify her and asked, 'What the fuck do you mean? How can there be a spark missing when we're both here, having so much fun? You're drunk, baby, that's all!' In the attempt to calm her down, I raised my voice.

'Hey! Why are you talking to me like this? Calm down! All I did was to ask if you actually love me or not. Have I offended you by asking this?'

Even though she replied in the sweetest voice possible, to my ears she sounded rude. 'Look, Radhika, don't you dare talk to me like that!' I pointed a finger towards her, which was my way of calming people down. As the argument heated up, she retreated to the adjacent seat, pulling up her denims, and looked pensively outside the window. This is a tact used by most girls when they want their boyfriends to win them over with some captivating one-liners. Though I was in no mood to entertain her, I had to bring the situation under control.

'Okay, Radhika, my baby! Listen to me. Just tell me, who the hell knows what this word "love" really means? I have been searching for its meaning for many years. Do you expect me to shout out my feelings for you from a hilltop? Will the multiple echoes multiply my love for you? Or should I run in the hayfields with a guitar in my hand and sing out to you?' I chuckled and winked.

'Aarav, why do you always have to end conversations like this? You think it's funny? It's not! Love is a very pure feeling. It involves two people caring about each other and understanding each other. But look at us. Do we seem like we're in a relationship? The emotion that lingers between us is LUST,' she said. 'We are together, not for each other, but for the physical satisfaction that we provide to each other. Don't you think we're a couple only on social media platforms, while in reality we don't give a damn about each other's emotions? We don't understand each other; there's no love, just lust.' There was sadness in her voice. This was the first time I was seeing in her eyes a burning passion for me. The car's air conditioning was still on, but suddenly, I felt hot and stuffy, like someone was holding me by my throat. The Radhika before me was no more the Radhika I knew three months before college started.

Radhika was my most recent fling. I had come in contact with her via Facebook. Finding 'love' was the easiest thing in today's time. All you needed was a Facebook account with a hot picture that had been duly Photoshopped, and you could land yourself a new 'love' in no time. Unfortunately, she made it to my college. Fortunately, she had taken business administration, not technology like me. Both officially and unofficially, I was her senior. We started hanging around soon after she joined, but she told me to keep our relationship a secret in college. I wonder why girls are so overprotective about such insignificant things. Anyway, we never talked about personal matters or tried to get to know each other intimately. Our interactions were limited to intertwined fingers, holding hands, cuddling and all that jazz.

To an extent, I did agree with what she was saying, but the question that arose in my mind was 'Why now?'

Her innocent question puzzled me, maybe because I'd never cared about her too much, or let myself get too attached to her. I was a part of all this just for my sexual gratification. I was totally baffled and didn't know what to say. Still, I tried a perfect reply.

'But you knew from the very beginning it was never anything serious. Why now?' I asked her again. Somehow, I was unable to look into her eyes.

'What? Should I *ask* you to love me? Shouldn't it come naturally to you?'

'But I *do* love you,' I almost pleaded this time.

'But I can't see it. I can't feel it. I can just hear you say those empty words. They lack any sign of emotions. That's all I have to say.'

I was getting very irritated with this conversation.

'How can a man who doesn't even know what love is, make a girl feel loved? Happiness to you is about getting drunk, love to you is lust, I feel like an idiot talking to you about this. You better go and learn what love is, but I am just so very sure that a man like you will never experience this beautiful feeling. Ever!' She threw her hands up in the air.

I had nothing to say to her anymore. Her words choked me up. I looked away from her. Somehow, I struggled to stop myself from crying. Had she seen my tears, she would have laughed at me, and I didn't want to give her that pleasure. Her words had left me speechless, but I still wanted to settle the sweltering debate.

'Look, sweetheart, we're spending such a great time together; ain't this enough?' I tried to persuade her. She was such a bimbo.

'Okay, then tell me one thing, does our relationship have any future, Aarav?' I was now tired of answering such questions. I stayed quiet. 'Then what next?' she asked, fuming.

She kept accusing me, and got it right sometimes.

'What the fuck do you think of yourself, huh? Am I just another whore for you to fuck every time you get a hard-on?' The tip of her nose had turned red and her eyes were bloodshot.

'Hey, mind your words, girl! Did I . . .' I screamed and raised one hand. I realized I looked like I was about to hit her, but I had no intention of physically hurting her.

'Did I what? Blurt out whatever you have in your mind! You want to hit me? Hit me then!' she said, bringing her face close to mine. Her voice broke and a tear dropped from her right eye.

'Let it be,' I murmured in irritation. 'Did I ask you to fall in love with me? Did I force you to come out this late with me to a deserted parking area, just so we could make out? You wanted it as much as me, so don't pretend otherwise. Look, I did NOT sign a contract saying, "I will love you forever" or "We will have two kids after marriage". Grow up, Radhika! I have always pampered you with the finest things—the latest dresses and accessories, chocolates and even your lingerie have been financed out of my wallet, girl!' I paused to breathe. Her face flushed with a rare shade of red.

'Do I not love you? Isn't this love, huh? Have I not supported you when you asked me to? Have I not amused you every single moment we were together? Now just wipe away your tears. I can't see you crying!' I said sharply.

Girls never do what they are told. In fact, they do exactly the opposite. She burst into tears.

'Okay, then let it be; live your life and I'll live mine. Go, find yourself a new lover, but don't create a scene over here,' I said roughly. She stared at me like a lost puppy. 'You'll never understand what love is Aarav. Never!'

She wiped away the tears, picked up her stilettoes and stormed out of the car. Watching her walk away, I promised myself I would never fall for a girl, *ever*. Someone rightly said, 'Let go of what you can't change, because life goes on anyhow!'

My eyes followed her until she turned around to look at me. It felt like a scene straight out of a romantic Bollywood flick. However, unlike those love stories where everyone gets their perfect someone in the end, this was reality.

I looked away and pulled out from under my seat my true love—a bottle of Jack Daniels whisky.

This wasn't a new situation for me. I had been with many girls in the past—some for weeks, some for days, and some for even just a few hours. I wondered how Radhika had lasted for more than a month. By god's grace, I was single again, ready to mingle. This relationship had ended in a pretty dirty way, but I guess, she deserved it for being so senseless.

For some strange reason, this time the break-up made me feel emotionally hurt. So while my heart ached, my head told me to be a man and get my act together. And with my Jack Daniels for company, I hoped getting over her won't be so difficult.

The whisky started working its magic on me and I started to lose my grip. Feelings and memories that I had buried deep inside me months ago started to reappear. I didn't feel like going back home that night. I parked my car at a secluded spot a few kilometres from my house.

It was around 8.30 p.m. I had received no call from my mum. I turned on the music player. I felt shattered, weak and lost. As the whisky took its toll on me, memories of my time with Anamika flashed in front of my eyes.

I had started to miss her. This happened to me every time I would gulp down more than two glasses of whisky at a time. With each sip, a new memory would present itself in front of me. Her face, her smile, her fondness for me . . . I don't know why, but even after the break-up, she was ruling my heart and mind.

I got out of the car with the bottle in my hand and started hurling abuses, even though there was no one around. As I gulped down the last sip, I took out my phone from my jeans pocket and saw there were nine missed calls—all from mom. I looked at the time on my watch. It was 11.00 p.m. I was too drunk to drive. With a thud, I crashed to the ground, looking around for someone to take me home, but the streets were deserted. I hoisted myself up and went straight towards my car. I fell down again in the middle of the street. Thankfully, there were no vehicles on the road. An ice cream seller came running towards me from a distance and helped me get back on my feet. '*Kya hua beta, theek tho ho?*' he asked. His voice seemed to echo from another galaxy. I was so wasted that I thought it best not to go home in such a state. I tossed the man's hand away and opened the door to the car. Once in, I turned on the ignition and drove at full speed, even though I was directionless.

* * *

I was driving recklessly at a speed of fifty kilometres an hour. Whisky makes men do totally outrageous things. I reached home. I was reeking of alcohol. It was an unpleasant odour for a teetotaller. I tiptoed to the entrance and knocked lightly on the door.

Thankfully, it was my sister, and not my parents. She opened the door. I tried to stand erect so as to hide the fact that I was badly drunk. She looked at me from top to bottom with utter disgust on her face. The whiff of the whisky was too strong to be shielded from her.

'Are you drunk? Mom! Look, here's your dear child at the door, completely drunk!' she screamed out. I wasn't in my senses and muttered, 'Bartender, a single malt whisky, quick! The first one didn't satiate my thirst, you know. Make it fast! Otherwise, I'll call the manager of this bar.'

'Bar?! Are you nuts or what? Wake up,' she rebuked, almost pushing me this time. By then, our parents had come out.

'What happened, Vaibhavi, why are you screaming so loudly? Do you know what time it is?' my mum asked, rubbing her eyes. She was still groggy from sleep.

'Mum, screams are supposed to be loud.' I chuckled.

'Look at this shameless guy. First, he arrives home so late, and second, he's drunk out of his mind.'

'And third, I want at least three reasons,' I said and giggled again, unaware that I was digging my own grave.

'My god! Look at his nerves. What a disgrace you are, boy! And if I may ask, where have you been for so long?' It was my dad this time, like a cop newly arrived at a crime scene. He was forgetting I was still playing the lead role here.

'Answer me, I am asking something,' he quizzed again. His interrogation style reminded me of ACP Pradyuman from the show *CID*. But I have to admit that he's a terrific father who really cares about me. He's a BITS Pilani alumnus, while I was not even eligible to appear for its entrance test. But he has never held this against me. He has always supported me in whatever I wished to do and encouraged me even when I failed—that said, I've failed him miserably as a son.

'Sir, all that I've done is asking for a drink. These bartenders here need to be taught some hospitality etiquette. Just give me one drink and I promise to pay and leave, ACP Pradyuman,' I muttered.

Dad couldn't take my nonsense any more. Perhaps I had crossed the threshold of his patience. In fact, I had demolished it.

He gave me a tight slap on my face that almost sent me flying. Seeing this, mother started crying. Her loud wail and the commotion we were creating woke up the neighbours. I saw a few aunties peeping out from their windows, trying to catch all the live action. It was late night, but it's never too late for pesky neighbours to meddle into other people's affairs.

The aunties had got enough masala for their kitty parties. I had put my parents to shame in front of the whole neighbourhood. And this was not the first time. To bring the whole drama to a halt, my father held me by the collar and dragged me in, while mother, in true-blue Bollywood fashion, cried out a well-known one-liner from old Hindi movies: '*Yeh din dekhne se pehle tune mujhey uthaa kyun ni liya, Bhagwaan!*'

I was an endless source of embarrassment for her. 'God didn't want melodrama in heaven, Mom, so he sent you here.' Even the word 'shameless' would have felt ashamed of me. I had now crossed all limits. Dejectedly, my parents and sister walked back to their bedrooms and shut the door.

Whisky kills you slowly. It hadn't just caused me harm in my present, it was going to do a lot more damage in the future, since I was soon to be disposed of my father's wealth and property.

I retreated to my bedroom and crashed on the pillow. The bed felt cold, as if I was lying on a slab of ice on a cold winter night. Even though I was in the comfort of my room, I felt like a dog who had been kicked out of the house by its owner.

But I deserved to sleep like a dog, to be treated like a dog. I wished I were a dog. I just needed a bitch by my side.

There's No Way Out

The worst part about a drunken night is that you have to face its consequences the next morning, especially when it involved creating a huge scene when you got back home. An aspirin later, all the memories come rushing back: the huge quantity of alcohol I gulped down, the terrible way I behaved and the terrible things I said. Even if I had forgotten a tiny detail, my family would make sure to remind me of all the things that I had done. I got up at around 10 a.m., after completely exploiting the snooze option on my alarm clock. But even after last night's debacle, I had the nerve to get out of my room and scream for breakfast. When I got no reply, I slowly trudged to the dining table. My sister was there, setting a plate for herself.

'Serve me breakfast,' I commanded.

She gave me an angry stare.

'What would you like to have, sir? Vodka with Sprite? Or should I call for wine this time?' she said, gritting her teeth in anger.

I shot back an angry look and strode towards the fridge.

It was empty!

What the fuck!

'Will anyone tell me why am I being subjected to such brutal behaviour?' I asked, infuriated.

'Why don't you ask the ACP, sir?' she retorted instantly.

I growled and left for college.

As I stepped out of the main door, I saw three of the neighbourhood aunties standing outside, whispering to each other.

As I passed them, I heard one say, 'What a waste of good upbringing! He is extremely shameless, Mrs Gupta, I was about to appoint him as my daughter's tutor . . .'

She stopped short as I neared her.

'Oh! You want me to tutor your lovely daughter, is it? But will she find the time for tuitions, considering she's always at her favourite pub, Reverb, drunk out of her senses? Even the bouncer at the pub knows her really well. She dances beautifully when high. Maybe she can give me some dance lessons in exchange for the tuitions?' I spat out and walked away.

The frustration of a bad morning may spoil the rest of the day. No breakfast, a crabby sister and gossipy neighbours are enough to make you feel helpless. But I told my brain to think of happy things.

On my way, I was greeted by many curious eyes, and that worsened my frame of mind. My parents have, over the years, told me to abide by the rules set by our 'society'. It is not me who decides how to live my life, society does. Right and wrong are no more moral issues, rather, they are the privileges of society. These self-proclaimed guardians of society are seriously messing up the lives of frivolous youngsters like me.

To add to my misery, the Delhi metro went at a snail's pace, halting time and again between stations, irritating the hell out of me.

'The next station is Punjabi Bagh,' came the metro announcement.

I heaved a sigh of relief when my destination arrived, but my relief was short-lived. At the entrance to the college's engineering wing, stood Radhika with swollen eyes. She had purposefully applied no kohl on her eyes to highlight their puffiness. Beside her stood the hunk of the business administration wing—Debashish Sen. He was a good-looking Bengali with a nice dressing sense and good physique. Girls found his dimples pretty electrifying. He was quite a geek and also a bookworm. He despised me for being in a relationship with Radhika. Radhika had once told me how he had asked her if they could be 'more than friends'. I remember how it had made me roll on the floor with laughter.

He had bent down on his knees, taken Radhika's hand, and said, *'Kya aap humaare bachho ko sagey bhai behen banne ka mauka dengi?'* How corny!

Now that Radhika and I had split up, he could swoop in and easily take my place. He strode towards me like a Bollywood villain. Eye contact was established. He narrowed his eyes at me. I gave back an ugly stare.

There was tension in the air. I flexed my fingers in my jeans pocket, ready to land a blow on his face. Heaven knows how hard I wanted to hit him that moment.

He growled and . . . *aaaannnchhooo*!

He sneezed.

I managed not to laugh.

'So, you want to be bashed up?' Deb made a poor attempt at threatening me.

'I believe in application rather than theory, you asshole!' I snarled and gave a smack on his dimpled cheek.

He looked dazed. I had no intentions of killing him; I had better things to do with my time.

I pointed a finger at him. Not the index or the pinkie, or the ring or the thumb, it's the one you show when you don't give a fuck.

He stepped back.

From the corner of my eye, I noticed him comforting Radhika and trying to wipe away her tears. Most girls come with a tap that lets out endless drops of tears at any given opportunity.

I walked with an air of confidence and entered my classroom. It was now Professor Talwar's chance to take a dig at me.

'Look, the college's cool dude is here. Welcome him, my friends,' he mocked.

'Please continue, sir, no formalities,' I smirked.

'Get out of my class, you spoilt brat! You're good-for-nothing! You think you can enter my class half-an-hour late and I'd let you get off easily?'

'I'm not late. I'm early for the next lecture,' I said and made a face.

The whole class giggled as Professor Talwar scowled. This particular professor held a lot of grudges against me. I had tried to be in his good books in the beginning, but seeing there was no point in that, I started giving it back to him—it was so much more fun!

The college was in complete chaos those days. Every student was either busy in organizing an event or in coordinating some activity to earn rubbish credentials. I was busy hunting for some good-looking Delhi University chicks who had turned up in our campus for a lacklustre carnival. After a long, hectic month of completing ludicrous assessments, it was time to have some fun.

Everyone was busy putting the finishing touches to their respective acts, while Karan and I were just lazing about. Karan Arora, my best buddy, was a bulky guy with no brains. He kept falling prey to even the silliest of bullies for no reason. Nobody knew him better than me. We had been besties since our high school days.

Some pretty hot chicks hung around the college premises. I was so bored of the girls from our college. We sat on a bench which gave us a clear view of the hotties arriving at our college. When the girls walked by, we would rate them from one to ten depending upon how hot they were. No one got went beyond six.

Suddenly, I noticed a familiar face in the crowd. A slim girl, dressed in a body-hugging charcoal-grey top and denims, pulled out a pencil from behind her ear as she instructed a volunteer about some event's chores. She was definitely a seven, or even an eight, if you ask me!

Oh, fish! MISHKA! Small world!

Mishka Narula and I had studied together till tenth standard after which we had changed our schools. She had willingly done it due to a tiff with her guy, while I had changed it unwillingly. Parental care, you know. They wanted me to study in some remarkable high school, even though I didn't want to. Mishka and I used to be great friends in school, but had lost touch after we both went our separate ways. I knew she was friends with Radhika; the bitch had told me once.

For a moment, I thought of walking up to her and saying 'hi'. Then I noticed her approaching my foe—Deb.

'WOAH! Is she dating that loser?' I wondered, although I didn't give a damn.

I turned back and tried to focus on something else.

From the corner of my eye, I noticed Deb and Radhika greeting Mishka like they were best friends with her. I made momentary eye contact with Radhika. Deb was standing right behind her like a bodyguard.

Mishka suddenly raised her hand to call out for me. Radhika nudged her and whispered something. Girls! I tell you. They are faster than the Indian media when it comes to spreading a tale. Mishka, who just a second ago seemed pleased to see me, now gave me a look of disgust. I didn't bother to greet her and walked out of that event with Karan.

The best part of the college carnival was the platinum opportunity to soothe your eyes with the best of god's creation—girls of all shapes and sizes, all colours and height, dressed in their best to draw the attention of admirers of beauty like me. I must have been looking pretty handsome that day. I noticed many hot chicks eyeing me every now and then. Desperate singles like me!

'Hiiiiiii . . . Aarav!' a familiar voice jerked me out of my thoughts. I turned around and found Mishka looking at me in a confused manner.

'Oh! Hi.' I was at a loss for words. Actually, I didn't want to start any conversation with her that would lead me to Radhika.

'How have you been? Changed so much, eh?' she taunted.

'Change is the rule of life,' I said rudely. 'Excuse me, I need to go.'

'Wait! I need to talk!' she exclaimed.

'What?' I said, avoiding any eye contact with her.

'I need to know why you did this to Radhika.'

'Why the fuck am I answerable to you?' I retorted.

'Is this how you talk to an old friend?' Her tone softened.

'This is how I am now. You got a problem? If you have, then don't talk to me.' Arrogance ruled my voice.

'You used to be such a reserved and decent guy, what has become of you, Aarav?' she said, stressing on the word 'decent'—a sort of emotional blackmail; but I had no intention of falling for it.

'I need to go!' I said and walked towards my gang. She ran after me and held my elbow.

'But I need to know why. I'm having a hard time believing the things Radhika has told me. If not now, then whenever you want.'

'How about never?' I said, as I jerked her hand away. I walked through the crowd, while a dozen memories of my secondary school years hovered in my mind.

'Oh, I'm sorry!' a sweet voice apologized as I felt something scorching my skin. 'Owww, fuck man!' I uttered as I turned around in disgust. A lovely lady, dressed in a black off-shoulder top and blue denim miniskirt gave me an apologetic smile. She had spilt her hot chocolate on me.

'The pleasure is all mine!' I spoke, elongating each and every word as I assessed her from top to bottom.

'Sorry?' she said, laughing at my reply. A hand suddenly went around her waist as I took the napkin from her.

'I just spilt my hot chocolate,' she said in a childish tone to the guy who had pulled her towards himself.

That's probably her boyfriend. Why are all hot girls committed to such puppies? I thought to myself.

I stood there mesmerized, staring at her full, juicy lips that had been painted with a pink lip gloss.

'Come, let's get you another one, love,' said that bastard and he kissed her. My gaze followed her sexy legs. I wondered how, in this cold winter, girls could be comfortable dressed in such scanty clothing.

'She's gone. Hot one, eh?' I said as Karan punched my shoulder.

'Darn! Her curves have ruined you . . .' Karan winked at me.

'Eyes,' I added, as we both laughed hard.

I enjoyed the company of this asshole. Then I wiped away the hot chocolate from my jacket.

In the evening, the war of DJs, more girls, and much more awaited us. My party-freak gang soon joined me. I grabbed a bottle of whisky from Karan and we were ready for a grand bash.

As we made our way to the venue, my phone vibrated. It was an unfamiliar number, so I disconnected.

We partied hard that night. At around two in the morning, I checked my phone again and saw there were five missed calls from the same number.

I texted my sister that I'd stay at my friend's place for the night. As if informing her mattered at 2 a.m.

We went to Raman's house to spend the rest of the night.

When I regained my senses, my head was resting on a hairy chest. 'Whose darn bed is this? Why are you in your boxers? Bloody hell! Why am I only in my boxers?' I panicked.

'Hey, hey! Chillax! I've not raped you,' said Raman as he grabbed his pillow, turned around and snored. He slid his hand down to scratch his filthy ass. I rubbed my eyes and let out a loud yawn. Karan was fast asleep on the floor.

I looked for my clothes, put them on and walked out of the bedroom. As I was about to pick up my phone from the living room, it rang. It was the same number. Then the battery died. I drove towards hell—my home!

* * *

The best thing about reaching home at noon was that I had to only face mom. It is far easier to tolerate her when dad isn't around. She speaks and I ignore her, easy enough. But perhaps, god was feeling really generous that day. Even mom wasn't home. She had gone for her kitty party.

I entered the house through the back and made a dash for the fridge. Gobbling up a sandwich, I plugged my phone in for charging. It rang again.

'Hello, who's this?' I said in a charming tone, expecting a hot chick at the other end.

'Hi, Aarav, does it cost you a million dollars to pick up a call?'

'Who's this?' I repeated.

'Mishka this side, can I have a few precious minutes of your day, sir?'

'What is it, Mishka?' I asked, annoyed.

'I want to meet you.'

How straightforward! This is how she was. Different from other girls in the sense that she never was up for long, useless conversations; she stuck to what was meaningful.

'I have a busy schedule this week.'

'I never said that meeting you next week is a problem for me.'

'Let me see, okay, bye.' I hung up.

This brief conversation with Mishka made my stomach twitch. Maybe it had to do with something called 'guilt'. But I thought I had become immune to being guilty for breaking up with bimbos.

'Aaargh!' I roared and threw the rest of my sandwich away. Suddenly I had lost my appetite.

A text beeped on my phone:

Derz no point in avoidin me . . . m not here 2 make u feel guilty or 2 shower lectures on u . . . jus wana talk 2 u . . . I xpct a rply –Mishka luk Mishka, I seriously don't wana discuss anything, leave me alone . . . u r no1 to sudnly cm n make a mess of my life lik that . . . so jus mind ur own chuffin busness

That is what I wanted to reply, but I didn't.

But if she doesn't want to make me feel guilty, why is she so desperate to have a word with me? The question boggled my mind. I strode up and down my room, pulled the curtains, jumped up and down the sofa, browsed through television channels, but the restlessness didn't pass.

The doorbell rang. Was it Mishka? Has she now tracked my house? I stumbled twice before I grabbed the door knob and opened it enough to peep through.

To my relief, it was just my lovely mom.

She looked like a fierce version of an Indian police officer ready to sputter interrogative questions at me about my absence from the house. I could visualize her dressed in a khaki uniform, tapping her stick and eyeing me with a raised eyebrow.

'Oh, Mom! It's you! I'm so glad you're back! I'm so damn hungry, get something to calm my belly down.' I made a modest attempt to distract her from the list of questions she was preparing in her mind.

A mother is the epitome of care. She forgets everything once her child cries with hunger.

Well, this was just an assumption of my splendid mind.

'Do you want me to pack your bags and throw you out along with them or will you do it yourself?' she shouted loud enough to scare the pigeons away from our window.

Umm . . . my mom has other ways to show her love and care.

'I'm ashamed of having given birth to a drunkard like you. Your father has never touched alcohol all his life.'

Well, this was surely an exaggeration.

She sobbed and continued, 'I wonder if his blood still rushes through your veins. No! It's only alcohol. Did we raise you to witness such a day?' She plonked herself on the sofa and burst into tears. 'You've given our whole family a bad name. Every time I walk out of home, I know I will be picked on because of you. You are the burning topic everywhere. My friends bitch about you in front of me. First, you missed making it to the IIT for that girl and now, you're doing all this rubbish.'

My past was my real weakness. But mom would not have bothered about my follies if she was not so bothered about society. 'Calm down, Mom!' I reached out to her to hold her.

She responded with a tight slap on my face.

'Get lost! Live at whoever's place you want to,' she shouted and switched back to crying.

'I am so sorry, Mom,' I uttered my most-used phrase with a shameless smile and caught my mother's hand gently.

And my job was done. I saw her heart melting. I wiped her tears away and hugged her. I had mastered the field of female psychology by now. I could handle any of them pretty easily.

I stayed home all day.

I tried to kill time on Facebook, gaming, staring at walls, trying to discover new angles of lying on my couch to have a better view of my ceiling fan, and so on.

My phone rang.

Not Mishka! Not Mishka! Not Mishka!

'Hello!'

'Hello, Aarav! How are you?' It indeed was Mishka.

'I'm fine . . . so?'

'Do you like to party?'

'Yeah, who doesn't?' I exclaimed, but on realizing whom I was talking to, I calmed down and continued, 'But why?'

'Remember Devika?'

Why is she bringing up such random names?

'The girl who would stick by your side 24/7 in school?' Of course, I could never forget that girl. She had a crush on me, but she was too garrulous and nosey. Well, she had a cute smile.

'She is in the town for New Year celebrations.'

'In town? Didn't she go abroad for higher studies?'

While I was better than Devika in studies, still she was the one who got to go to a foreign university. The perks of being born to a rich family. Luck, what the fuck!

Mishka continued, 'Yeah . . . She's returning this week and throwing a New Year party—all friends are invited, she'd be just so happy to see you.'

'Oh wait! Who said I'm coming?'

'Of course, you are coming. No excuses! Farmhouse, chilling winter, bonfire, drinks, music! Eeeiiii! I'm so excited! And our first invitation goes to you. You can't turn it down like that.'

'Okay, I'll confirm in a day or two,' I replied in an exhausted tone and hung up.

Whoa! She hadn't uttered a word about Radhika.

Party . . . eh? I really needed a break from whatever was going on in my life. 'But if Mishka is coming . . . NO! That means Radhika is coming!' I shouted loud enough that my father heard.

'Alcohol not yet off your nerves, Mr Son of the ACP?' Dad commented.

I got up from the couch, went straight to my room and banged the door shut.

Life Goes On . . .

Karan, the asshole, woke me up with a call the next morning. 'How have you not been suspended yet? Get your ass to college and meet me in ten minutes.'

'Hmm . . . catch you in an hour.' I yawned and got up from the bed.

At college, it was a rather boring day, but took an eventful turn when I came across Deb.

'I'm going to set you right,' Deb challenged.

'Are you fucked up in the head or what?' I retorted, then turned to Raman and Karan, and continued, 'Deb's keema is going to be on the menu today.'

Deb tried to grab my collar.

Radhika came running and caught my arm. 'Leave him alone,' she nearly pleaded.

'You should have asked your pig-headed guy to stay away from me.' I pushed her hand away.

Deb punched me in the belly, but it felt like a tickle.

I clenched my fist to punch in response.

A crowd started gathering around for the free show. Only one of them, Mishka, had the courage to intervene. She made unsuccessful attempts to separate the two of us. Now the dean appeared, and the crowd dispersed. Deb, the coward, tried to hug me to escape suspension. I gave him a sharp blow on the ribs.

Suddenly, Deb fell on the ground.

'Deb!' Mishka shouted terrified. 'What happened to him?' she screamed at me.

Deb was lying on the ground, his mouth bleeding.

'He must have done something,' Radhika said accusingly.

'Help us get him to the doctor, you motherfuckers!' Mishka shouted at the crowd. I had never seen Mishka speak so aggressively.

Two boys stepped forward to help Deb into a car.

I was getting worried now.

'I'm gonna get your balls!' Radhika threatened me as she started dialling a number.

A few minutes later, I realized that she had called the police!

'This guy has issues with Deb. He has tried to hurt him before,' Radhika told one officer. There was no way out for me now.

The inspector held me by my collar.

'Another rich spoilt brat, aren't you?' the officer said wickedly. 'Aah! How I love dealing with such cases.'

He gave me a strange gaze, sizing me up. What's worse than being arrested is probably being handcuffed by a gay police officer.

'Bbbbbb . . . but you can't arrest me until that guy gives his statement. I haven't done anything except hug him back.' I stuttered and made an attempt to delay my trip to jail.

The inspector agreed and we headed to the hospital where Deb had been admitted. Mishka and Deb were already there. That day, for the second time in my life, I got an opportunity to ride in a PCR. Memories of the first ride came back to me as I got into the back seat with the havildar.

'Are you happy now?' Mishka shouted and gave me a look of disgust.

'Quiet, ma'am, please, it's a hospital.' A nurse came to my rescue followed by a doctor who came to inform us about Deb's condition. He had hurt his rib, but his condition was stable. The inspector was granted permission to visit him. There was no way to delay my arrest any further.

Deb was going to get back at me for everything, for every encounter with me, Radhika's break-up, his broken rib! I was in deep shit.

The inspector went into the ICU and came out after some 905 seconds. Yes, I was counting each and every second.

'The boy said he didn't want to file any complaint against Aarav. There was no fight, and Aarav didn't hurt him deliberately,' the officer declared.

'But, sir! I can get you so many witnesses against this guy,' Radhika spoke through her teeth.

'If Deb files no complaints against him, we cannot take any action. You're free to go, boy, but be careful in the future.' The officer left. I was too perplexed to react coherently. I felt my body being drained of something; I had gone totally numb. I rushed to the doctor.

'Can I meet him once?'

The doctor nodded and I ran into the room.

Mishka and Radhika followed right behind. Deb was lying on the bed with the oxygen mask and other apparatus that I had only seen once before in my life.

'Why did you do this favour to me?' my voice broke.

Deb opened his eyes and smiled.

'Because I am not Aarav.' His words were a mere whisper, but they echoed in my head. I stared at him in astonishment and my eyes became moist.

'He's not the guy I've known since childhood. I know people change, but do they change so drastically?' Mishka murmured rhetorically to Radhika.

Deb's forgiveness was perhaps his revenge.

His gesture had invoked in me a feeling that I had become invulnerable to—shame and guilt.

My knees could no longer bear my weight and I fell on the floor, my head held between my knees. My chest felt heavy.

A gentle hand rested on my shoulder. 'Are you okay?' Mishka inquired. Just then, the nurse entered. 'Let him rest. Move out, please.'

Mishka helped me get up. Radhika kept murmuring hateful words.

We went to the hospital cafeteria. I hadn't regained my bearings yet and the girls were sensible enough not to force me to speak.

'Ahem! Coffee?' Radhika asked.

I nodded my head in agreement. I gulped down the coffee at once and walked out of the cafeteria.

I had always longed to see Deb in this condition. What had happened to me now? Why was I being so affected by the situation?

Many classmates had gathered there. I could see hatred in their eyes for what I had done to Deb. They absolutely detested me for my evil deed. I felt their stares on me, but I wasn't able to look at any of them. I suddenly had a strong urge to meet Deb.

Hospitals always brought back some bad memories that I had deliberately pushed away from my mind.

I peeped through the ICU window to have a look at Deb. He was fast asleep. The nurse rushed to me to inform me that he was on anaesthesia. I turned back and found Radhika and Mishka in the corridor.

'Will he be all right?' I managed to ask, still not able to look them in the eyes.

'What do you . . .' Radhika fumed but Mishka restrained her.

'Yes, he'll be fine. I think you should go home. Your family must be worried about you,' said Mishka in an assuring tone.

I went and sat down on a bench without responding.

The day had exhausted me physically and mentally. I fell asleep sitting on the bench. I suddenly woke up when someone wrapped a shawl around my shoulders.

'Oh! I'm sorry I woke you up, son.' It was Deb's mother. She looked like a typical Indian mother. Her face reflected the pain of her son. 'How's Deb now?' The question came out of me involuntarily. 'I thought you had gone back to some pub to celebrate,' Radhika said sarcastically as she passed by.

I shrugged.

'Umm . . . well, Deb woke up a few minutes ago. He'll be discharged in about three days. By the way, you forgot your phone in the ICU. Your mum had called up a couple of times. I informed her that you were taking care of a friend in the hospital. She sounded like she didn't believe me. No one expects care and affection from you,' Radhika taunted, almost throwing the phone at my face, and left.

I went to the restroom and splashed some cold water on my face. I looked at the mirror. Was this the same guy I had seen earlier this morning? My phone buzzed again. It was mom.

'Hello. Yes, Mom?'

'Now which bar have you stationed yourself tonight? And who was that girl? She sounded too decent to be your friend.'

'MOM! My friend has met with a serious accident. I'm here with him at the hospital. I had dozed off for a while, which is why my friend attended the call. I'll be home as soon as things settle down here.'

'Are you okay?' Mom's voice suddenly softened.

'Yeah, Mom. Bye. Love you. Take care.'

'Huh? Come again?' She sounded astonished.

It had been really long since I bid goodbye to mom like that. 'Come on, Mom, I love you. Bye now.' I disconnected the phone and went back to the ICU. Mishka and Radhika were sitting beside Deb, cracking lame jokes to cheer him up.

'Ahem . . . well, may I join you guys?' I interrupted their chatter. There was silence for a while. Then Mishka stood up to offer me a place beside Deb.

'Yeah, why not! Come and sit here.' She had a welcoming smile.

I hesitated for a moment, but Deb gestured at me to sit near him.

'I . . . I'm . . . I mean . . .' I choked again on seeing the hospital apparatus.

Deb tried to pat my shoulder, and flinched with pain. I held his hand gently. Deb always reminded me of Kishnendu, and the relationship we shared.

'I'm sorry,' I finally spoke with tears in my eyes.

Radhika threw her hands up in the air in disgust. Mishka gave her an ugly stare.

Deb just smiled.

'Aarav was here the entire day for you.' Mishka made an attempt to defend me.

'And he was here the whole day because of me,' I spoke out of guilt and hung my head in shame.

'We'll be together from now on.' Deb chuckled. 'Friends?' he asked as he raised his hand towards me the way children do while making up after a fight.

Why is he so darn forgiving? His gestures were making me feel more guilty.

'Still holding some grudges, huh?' Deb winked at me.

'Nah!' I replied and shook his hand.

'Oww!' he screamed in pain.

'Oops! Sorry!' I gave an apologetic smile.

'I don't forgive you.' He suddenly became serious.

'I know it isn't easy for you,' I grimaced.

'Hey chill! I have a punishment for you.' The innocent smile returned. He winked at Mishka and Radhika who had been sitting quietly. Mishka winked back, while Radhika groaned.

'Anything, sir,' I replied like a sincere student.

'Anything?' he asked emphatically.

I nodded.

'Well, you have to spend the New Year with us.' He grinned.

'And?' I was waiting to hear what the punishment was.

'That's it. New Year's Eve with us. Our lovely friend is throwing a party at her farmhouse.'

'I've already told him; in fact, the first invitation went to him.' Mishka almost jumped in excitement.

'Oh! Great then! So it's done. This is your punishment, your act of contrition and all that crap!' Deb smirked.

'Ok, I'll come,' I said.

The nurse came to tell us that the doctor was about to visit, so we must leave the room.

'Take care, Deb,' I patted his hand gently and walked out behind Mishka and Radhika.

Deb's mother met us in the corridor. 'Thank you so much, beta, for being here at this difficult moment,' she said.

'Aunty, he's our friend. We care for him. Please don't thank us,' Radhika said and hugged her.

Deb's mother tried to hold back her tears but failed. Like the typical Indian mother, she was ruled by her emotions.

'You must all go home now. Your parents must be worried,' she expressed concern.

'Okay. But please let us know if you need anything, Aunty,' Mishka said, and we left.

'So, may I drop you both to your houses?' I tried to be chivalrous.

'We know the way to our homes,' Radhika said bitterly.

Then the girls communicated through their eyes. I was alien to this form of conversation.

After a while, Mishka said, 'Can you please drop us to my place?'

'Oh yes, sure.' I was eager to be of any help.

Then I realized that I didn't get my car to the hospital. I buzzed Karan to get his car to the hospital as soon as possible.

Karan was at our service within fifteen minutes.

The ladies got seated at the back and we drove towards our destination. We remained silent all through the way, except for Mishka's directions.

* * *

We reached Mishka's place in about twenty minutes

Mishka thanked us for dropping them off, while Radhika turned away pretending to make a call. We said our goodbyes to the girls, and I asked Karan to drop me to my place.

When we reached there, I hugged and thanked the ass for his help.

I went up to the door and rang the bell.

'So, you're back! Hammered again?' My crackbrained sister flared up as soon as she opened the door.

I ignored her, as always.

'Ewww! You smell like morphine.'

'Because hospitals don't offer whisky,' I replied rudely.

'Oh! I see. So, that friend's accident was not a work of fiction?' She kept provoking me.

'Why don't you just get married and pester your in-laws instead?'

I pulled her hair and poked at her forehead, and ran. She started chasing me. It had been so long since I had such playful brother–sister moments with her.

She finally caught up with me, grabbed me by my ear and dragged me to mom who was serving dinner. I followed her, crying out in pain and shouting, 'Ow! Ow!' till she released my ear.

'He's quite eager to get me married, Mom,' she said.

'I don't see a problem with that.' Mom winked at me and gave me a high-five!

My sister acted as if she was annoyed and then burst into laughter.

'I missed you so much,' she said as she ruffled my hair.

I wrapped my hand around her shoulder and cuddled her.

She was the most annoying girl in the world to me, but she was also the world's most lovable person.

Yes, I had changed. But what exactly had led to such a change, I still didn't know. Mishka was trying to figure out the same thing, I guess. Something felt fishy about her sudden invitation to the New Year party.

I had heard and was now experiencing how small incidents bring about huge changes in one's life. Who would have known that I'd spend such a joyous moment with my family this evening; that I'd be friends with my enemy, Deb; and that I'd spend an entire day without being intoxicated.

Well, life goes on . . .

New Year's Night!

I was sitting in the college canteen when I saw a girl approaching me. 'Oh, hi! Aarav? Don't recognize me? I'm Devika, yaar.' The attractive girl shook my hands.

It really was Devika! She was with Deb and Mishka.

'It's so good to see you. You haven't changed much, eh?' she said cutely.

'It's good to see you too. But you have changed a lot, Devika. I was not able to recognize you at first! Anyway, how have you been?' I asked with a wink.

'I've been great, but I miss you guys.'

'If you people are done talking, shall we proceed to the party? We are getting late,' Mishka interrupted. Deb was smiling. He was slowly recovering from the blow, and was trying to get back to his normal routine.

We chatted for a while and then made our way to the farmhouse for the much-awaited party.

Everything was set. The night was foggy, and the decorative lights added to the surreality of the scene. My body shivered due to the cold wind. Logs were ready to be lit. Food, drinks, music, everything created an enthralling effect.

'Whoa! Now this is something!' Deb exclaimed.

Friends had started to gather, and everybody was greeting each other warmly.

Karan and Raman came a little late.

'So, you decided to come after all, eh?' Karan said as I smiled at him.

There was a DJ playing in one corner, while everyone grooved to the music and drank to their heart's content. It was good to see old acquaintances gather in one place. I drank a lot, much more than I should have, as usual.

The music stopped for a minute. It was barely ten seconds to the New Year. Slowly, everyone started counting down to midnight . . . 10 . . . 9 . . . 8 . . . 7 . . . 6 . . . 5 . . . 4 . . . 3 . . . 2 . . . 1.

It was 12.00 a.m.! We were in 2011!

Greetings of 'Happy New Year' filled the air.

The music started again and it continued to become louder. I remember falling on the dance floor. Deb carried me to the couch.

Oops! I was drunk! I kissed Deb on his head.

'I love you, bro! I really do!' I shouted in my drunken state. We hugged each other!

It was getting colder. Some of the drunken party animals had started to disperse. Couples sat in corners kissing and cuddling each other.

Deb left me alone to get something to eat. While he was gone, I tried to steady myself to make sense of the world around me, even though my head was reeling.

A couple close by was in an animated conversation.

'My family won't allow it, we have no future together,' the girl said and broke down into tears. 'We need to separate. I am sorry. I love you. But this is just not possible. My family would die of shame,' she continued.

The guy was trying to calm her down. 'Please control yourself; you have to be happy, for my sake. Life doesn't stop. You have to live, you have to love.'

'Will you be able to love someone else?' The girl had nothing more to say and she walked away.

The guy seemed drained of life and I could see he was crying.

Even though I was struggling to stay upright, I tried to console the guy.

Tears trickled down my eyes. I patted his shoulder lightly and then hugged him. He whimpered.

'I sympathize with you, boy.'

By that time, Deb had returned with a plate of snacks. He caught me just as I was about to fall and apologized to the guy.

The moment took me back to my past. Everything was fresh and clear. Every memory that I thought I had erased came rushing back. I started breathing heavily.

Karan and Mishka too came to soothe me.

Deb arranged a couch for me near the bonfire.

It was about 2.00 a.m. Almost everyone had left.

We were too tired to move. I couldn't stop my tears from flowing.

Mishka finally gathered the nerve to ask me why I was crying.

'What is troubling you, Aarav?' she asked in a low voice.

'Nothing.'

'C'mon, Aarav, we're friends. You can share anything you want with us. You'll feel better, I promise!' Deb exclaimed.

'It isn't a single event, it's an entire chapter of my life that taught me to love, to live . . . I was the happiest person in the universe, but destiny had something else in store for me. And then everything changed . . . I was deprived of her . . . of everything . . . it was the darkest phase of my life.'

Everyone had their eyes glued on me. I was bawling.

'Alcohol has taken over his senses.' I could hear Devika say.

Everyone ignored her.

'Can you please be a bit more clear?' Deb demanded.

'I don't have the courage to live those moments again. I have been running away from them for a long time. I beg you to not ask me to remember what I want to forget,' I asserted. Then my tears resumed flowing.

Everyone started insisting I reveal the true cause of my misery, and in the end, I was left with no choice.

Deb put an arm around me and said, 'No one can force you. If you are comfortable with telling your story, we're all ears. If not, that's okay too.'

I had no intention of turning down their requests now.

I cleared my throat. Everyone settled around the bonfire and looked eagerly at me. For a moment, I felt like an old grandma narrating a story to her grandchildren.

I looked into the bonfire, trying to remember it all, and began: 'Yes, I had a love story . . . I fell for someone . . . she was my love, my life, the most beautiful creation of the almighty . . . my angel, Anamika!' My voice broke. 'This is what you were asking for, Mishka. You'll get your answers today!'

First Glimpse

2 July 2008. It was the first day at my new school. I had scored 'pretty average' marks in my secondary school exams. Well, 88.7 per cent was considered a 'pretty average' score in my family. But I had to change my school as my father wanted me to study in a reputed institution. So I was dragged away from my friends.

That day, I felt like a primary school kid, unwillingly sent to an alien place.

I had reached school in time so as to make a good impression on the teachers on my first day. I was missing my previous school and friends terribly. To make matters worse for me, I had taken up the sciences. Everything was making me anxious. I felt an urge to run away. I wasn't really sociable, so I couldn't gather the courage to introduce myself and make friends with the people around me. *What if they say, 'No, we can't be friends with you'?* I felt they should have been courteous enough to help me feel comfortable on my first day.

Friends hugged each other as they were meeting after the long summer break. But I had no one to talk to. This made me paranoid.

8.00 a.m. An announcement boomed through the halls. Everyone started leaving their classrooms with diaries in their hands.

'Hey, you don't look concerned at all about the assembly, eh?' a chirpy voice asked.

It was Rahul, a tall, dark and handsome Jat boy, as tall as a Lakers' basketball player.

'No, actually I don't have a diary with me. I am a newcomer,' I mumbled. 'By the way, I am Aarav,' I added with a smile, offering my hand to him.

'Hi, I am Rahul, the prefect of eighth standard,' he said with some pride.

We both left hurriedly for the assembly hall. The 'prefect' had disappeared among the thick maze of students. I remembered my father's clichéd advice: *'Beta, dost-vost sab sath chhor dete hai musibat ke samay.'* My head was filled with such thoughts as I looked around me to find a place to stand. Finally, I recognized a few faces from my class and stood in a file behind them.

The morning prayers commenced, followed by a welcome speech by the principal. I looked up at the sky—dark grey clouds were bursting at the seams and it seemed like they would start crying any time to sympathize with me. Meanwhile, our class prefect started inspecting our uniforms. I looked around for Rahul, but couldn't spot him anywhere despite him being taller than anyone else in the hall. My father's words were ringing in my head, again.

Just then, I heard the voice of a girl carrying out the inspection of our row of students. She started getting students out from the queue due to faults like long nails, dirty shoes, missing school belt, wrong tie, no diary . . .

Her voice was as soothing as that of a nightingale. The moment she came to me, I turned my head to look her straight in the eyes. She was almost four inches shorter than me, so I had to look down into her eyes. A tremor rushed through my body. Those twinkling eyes were trying to ask something, but I had no answers to give.

I was left gaping at her, struggling to find my breath. She was a rare beauty. She was not too fair, nor did she have long hair. A frame of thick-black spectacles covered her beautiful brown eyes. She had tied her hair into a ponytail. She had a small nose, red lips, and a mole above her upper lip like Cindy Crawford.

We both stood looking at each other. I could not move, my body was almost paralysed. This was the first time my heart skipped a beat on seeing a girl. Maybe it was because I was standing so close to a girl after such a long time. The last time I had come so close to a girl was in the sixth standard. We had both tried to kiss for the first time, but it had ended disastrously. She told me she'd get pregnant if we kissed for more than five seconds. Prepuberty days are the silliest, yet the most beautiful days of one's life.

She looked at me—from my hair to my shoes—keenly.

Was I looking handsome?

Was she impressed?

I wouldn't dare open my mouth, in case I had bad breath.

It was my tendency to get sweaty every time I faced a tense situation. My body froze whenever someone looked straight into my eyes and questioned me. She was doing the same thing. A badge pinned to her right pocket gave away her name and designation—Anamika Roy: Prefect, XI standard. I read 'Prefect' as 'Perfect'.

'Where is your diary?', she asked, inspecting me again from top to bottom. 'Show me your hands,' she inquired in her saccharine-sweet voice as she looked at my nails.

'Umm . . . err . . . actually . . .' Being the shy person I was, I was struggling for words.

'Oh! So you're not carrying your diary, is it?' she asked, as if she was going to give me third-degree torture for such a minor error. It was a big school with thousands of students. I didn't expect her to recognize that I was a new student.

She held my hand and took me out of the queue to present me in front of the teacher in charge of discipline. As soon as she grasped my hand, I felt something magical, something out of the ordinary.

As soon as she let go of my hand, the magic vanished, but the sensation lingered for a while. We both looked at the sky together. It had started to drizzle. I was not yet out of the spell of Miss Perfect.

It started raining hard. Everyone was running helter-skelter for cover. I had never been too fond of rains. But today, I didn't mind it one bit.

Miss Perfect was carrying an umbrella. She was standing only a few inches away from me and her hands brushed against mine several times. If her standing beside me was making my heart go wild, these brushes would make it stop beating!

She tried to tuck her hair into her shirt even as she was opening the umbrella. She looked so sweet and innocent. The wind would not let her umbrella open. It was clear she needed help, but she seemed too proud to ask for it. I took the umbrella from her and opened it with ease, looking straight into her eyes.

She took the umbrella from me and ran off. She didn't even consider offering me the umbrella. Indifferent and insensitive she was, but despite all that, she was totally adorable.

She might have gone, but only from my sight. She had pierced her way into my heart. My world was no longer the same. The ground under me had shifted.

By the time I became aware of myself and my surroundings, I was drenched and my clothes were almost transparent.

As I left for my class, the incident played over and over again in my mind.

But that was the only interaction I was to have with her for the next whole year.

After that, I did not have any conversation with Anamika except for the occasional 'excuse me' whenever she came to our class to meet her friends. I saw her quite often, sometimes alone, other times with friends. I noticed her every time, but I could never muster the guts to talk to her. Later, I started keeping myself away from her and her friends.

Days passed in the torture that was science. My mother had forced me to take up science, so that I could crack the IIT entrance test. But I had always wanted to be a newsperson. That year passed in a blur of question banks and lonesomeness. Soon, I started losing contact with my old school friends, even with some of my best friends. Everything was changing at a fast pace. I didn't even have time to think where I was heading.

My life had become colourless. No outings, no parties, not even good friends. I missed my old friends. Even though we met on some Sundays, it was not even close to the fun we used to have together. We were all changing. But somewhere deep inside, we knew we loved and cared for each other.

I had made many good friends. Good enough to be invited to birthday parties, to go out with, to hang out for drinks, and good enough to teach you to have a better perspective towards life.

Schooldays

When you are growing up, you do not realize how fast things change. And before I knew it, it was time for my eighteenth birthday.

Birthdays often bring you in the limelight and make you feel special. It is almost always a big day for the person whose birthday it is, but it might also be special for others who are close to that person. You are excited about the gifts, blessings and birthday wishes you are about to receive, while others are often excited about the treat they might receive on this special occasion. Officially, I was turning eighteen today, having already witnessed many things in my life. This was the time when Orkut had been murdered by Facebook. This was the time when girls were no longer cautious about wearing shorts and skirts. This was also the time when people preferred Subway over McDonald's, and Pizza Hut over Domino's. Laptops had taken the place of assembled PCs. It was a usual morning that day.

Our break had just started. I took Rahul, Karan, Oshit (popularly known as Oh-shit), and Aniket to our canteen, named 'Gulshan da Adda' by the seniors.

Luckily, we got seats—not a small accomplishment considering how tiny the place was. I remembered my last birthday when there were some twenty students with me who made me stand on a table in the school canteen which was larger than this. Everyone sang the birthday song for me. I had felt very special. I was missing them this morning. We hadn't lost our friendship, but we had lost touch. I managed to paste a fake smile on my face while ordering Gulshan's Special Thali for the gluttons. That was the only 'special' thing that had happened to me on that day.

'So, what are the plans for today?' Aniket inquired.

Aniket was a happy-go-lucky guy. People often remarked that we looked like twins. His body structure, complexion and even his manner of interaction was similar to mine. The thing I loved about him was his straightforward attitude.

'Nothing much. I will just go out in the evening with some friends, and then a small dinner with family. That's it,' I replied nonchalantly.

The Jat boys, Oshit and Rahul, were busy enjoying their Coke. Only ten minutes of the break remained, but Karan, being the glutton that he was, wanted more food. He was a fatty with a decent amount of brains, but no skills to utilize it.

He had just one aim: to join some good engineering college. In other words, he was just a victim of his parents' dreams.

'Hey, just get me one more Coke and a grilled sandwich!'

'One for me too!'

'Hmmm, okay.'

I got them whatever they asked for.

'Anything else, guys?' It was customary to ask this question even if your pockets had run dry and there was nothing else you could afford. 'Anything else, guys?' I asked again.

A 'yes' would have put me in a difficult spot, but it seemed like the treat was over.

'Hey, guys! The notice for this year's school trip is out. Aarav, are you coming with us to Manali?' Aniket stressed the last word, so I would agree, but I didn't reply. Just then, the bell rang, and I went back to the counter and paid for the meals.

We hurried our way to class, skipping stairs in haste.

I saw Anamika there, conversing with her mates, Sunaina and Shanaya.

'They must have told her about my birthday,' I said to myself, hoping she would wish me.

We went straight to them as the teacher hadn't yet come. Anamika and Shanaya were still giggling about something one of them had said to the other. We were a huge group of friends, but I didn't frequent their outings.

'Here comes the birthday boy,' Sunaina said in a jovial tone, still not wishing me.

Anamika stood there smiling at me. Her brown eyes looked so deep and beautiful when they were not bespectacled. I had an intense yet awkward eye contact with her; intense for me, but probably awkward for her.

'Thanks,' I uttered in excitement while standing next to her. I could not see anyone around me at that moment. All my focus was on her. She was incredibly attractive—simple, yet exceptionally beautiful.

'But we haven't wished you yet!' The girls giggled in chorus.

Sunaina was very talkative. She could never stay quiet and had to speak even if she was not part of the conversation. Providing unsolicited advice and asking countless questions were the things she excelled at. She was Aniket's girlfriend.

'Happy birthday, Aarav!' Anamika said, taking my breath away. She then offered her hand. I gulped in nervousness. I had an adrenaline rush and my hands became sweaty. I hesitated before touching her beautiful hand with my filthy, sweaty one. But I just couldn't ignore it without seeming impolite. We shook hands. Shanaya was sitting in a seductive posture, with her legs crossed and her extremely short skirt giving a full view of her panties. The guys were ogling at her. Despite my state of mind, I too found myself staring at her for a few seconds. But I knew that it meant nothing.

Shanaya had unbearably sexy legs and voluptuous curves, and a soothing hazelnut complexion. An evident layer of make-up highlighted her heart-shaped face and made her cheekbones more prominent.

'Hmmm . . . Thanks Ana . . .' I tried to thank her, but at that very moment the teacher entered our class. Everybody around settled down. It was our physics teacher, Manju Kharbanda, who was perpetually shouting, irrespective of whether the class made any noise or not. Hence, the students preferred to not do anything to further agitate her.

She taught something about magnetism that day. I was just familiar with one magnetic attraction in the world—Anamika.

Anamika and Shanaya left for their classes. I had noticed Anamika smiling, looking back, but at whom or what I wasn't sure of. I just assumed it was me she was smiling at and I smiled back. Very insignificant for her perhaps, but very meaningful for me. This was our second proper interaction.

'Mr Aarav, would you please enlighten the class on ferromagnetism?' The abominable voice of the physics teacher shook me out of my bliss.

I stood up, looking around for help.

'You are constantly smiling in my class, and not paying attention. Would you just . . .'

'Ma'am, it's his birthday today.' My friends came to my rescue.

'Oh! So the birthday boy shall get special privileges today.' The teacher smiled. I smiled back as I had no idea how else to react. The bell rang and I heaved a sigh of relief. I couldn't concentrate on anything else the whole day—that 'Happy Birthday, Aarav' in that saccharine voice kept echoing in my ears all through, and the soft touch of her hand remained fresh in my mind.

Soon, that's how my time passed. Thinking about her and dreaming about all the possibilities that existed. In this haze, months passed by. We crammed for our exams as they came. The easy months at the beginning of the year gave way to a crucial time for the IIT aspirants. It was time for us to quit doing any extracurricular activities, and study with full concentration.

* * *

Before we knew it, the final exam of eleventh class was over. The day of the results arrived. I had scored a satisfactory 70 per cent, while Aniket had flunked two papers and Rahul in one. Sunaina had managed to clear all the papers while Anamika had topped her batch with 91 per cent. I was convinced that she had no boyfriend, because there was no way she could have scored this well with a partner in the picture. I consoled myself with this theory, even though I was painfully aware of its illogical nature.

Our parents had been called to school on the results day. This was when I saw her parents for the first time. I entered the classroom early with mom, not expecting many people at that time. But almost all my classmates were already there. I hurried to grab my mark sheet and left the room as quickly as possible. As I stepped out, I saw Anamika with her parents. Her parents confirmed all my stereotypes about Bengali parents. Her mom was wearing an off-white sari in the old-fashioned Bengali style, perfectly draped. She had a big red bindi on her forehead. Her father seemed comfortable in a shirt–trouser combination. He was a handsome man. Anamika had her mother's eyes and had gotten her cute little nose from her father. She had the best of both worlds. Their humble attitude towards everyone they came across was the only thing that Anamika had failed to acquire.

I tried to tell my mother about Anamika in order to know her opinion about her.

'Mom, our school topper, Anamika,' I said, pointing my finger at her. I had deliberately avoided using her full name, as that would have given away Anamika's Bengali origin. My mother had her silly prejudices against all flesh-eating Homo sapiens. I waited for my mother to react, but she completely ignored it, and said, making a face, 'Why are you not the topper of the batch?'

I thanked myself for not telling her Anamika's full name. Being the topper of the class had been enough to sow a seed of hatred for her in my mother's mind.

'Let's go,' she ordered and I followed.

'So, how was your result, son?' my dad asked, expecting something out of the ordinary.

'Must have flunked in two or three subjects,' Vaibhavi shrugged. As she was the firstborn in our family, I was compelled to give her some respect. Sometimes she truly deserved to be respected, but on some occasions, she annoyed me by being domineering.

'I got a 70 per cent,' I said proudly.

'Show me.' She snatched the report card from my hand in disbelief. I really like it when people don't expect anything good from me and I surprise them.

'Seventy per cent? It's 69.3 per cent. Exaggerating your scores is not a key to success,' she said mockingly.

'It's ok, it is not a big deal. When you pass out from IIT as a successful engineer, it'll shut her up,' my dad said hopefully.

The next few weeks passed in the hullabaloo of the Manali trip. No twelfth grader was expected to miss the trip, so I had no option.

Finally, we had some holidays to enjoy.

I daydreamed about the trip till the day finally arrived.

A Wimp in Love

My sister had started getting paranoid about my four-day trip. She was being overly considerate. I was getting lectures from everyone in the house on various things—on how to behave during the journey, about the cold weather in Manali, and about the whereabouts of my undergarments in my bag.

On the day of the trip while I was daydreaming, the phone rang. It was Akshay. 'Hey, get up and pack. I'll be there at 4.00 p.m. sharp in my new Skoda Fabia,' he said.

'Okay, no worries. I'll be ready,' I said and hung up.

I was too excited to go back to sleep, but somehow managed a few hours.

When I woke up, I began my preparations. I smeared some gel on my hair and sprayed deodorant on myself.

It was only 3.30 p.m., but Akshay was already there to pick me up.

'Hey, man, why are you so early? You were supposed to come at 4.00 p.m. in your *Skoda Fabia*, but I see it has undergone some drastic remodelling,' I taunted.

'Sorry, brother. I had to collect my Armani jacket before leaving from a friend, and my dad was not home yet, so I hurriedly brought my Maruti 800 AC.' Such a show-off.

I went inside my house to get my luggage, and returned with a worried mother and fussy sister.

'Take care and don't behave like a scamp there,' Vaibhavi said.

We finally left after an entire session of safety advice and goodbyes. Akshay's Maruti 800 'AC' was more like a furnace due to the scorching heat outside. We were both sweating profusely by the time we reached school and headed towards the reception.

We had been divided into groups, each travelling in a different bus. Our group had twenty members. I was familiar with only six of them. I saw Aniket, Karan and Sunaina standing together with their bags, and giggling.

'Hey, here comes the man,' Aniket shouted. He was looking good.

'Hey, man, ready to rock?' I asked, adding a fake laugh. I myself didn't feel like I was ready to rock.

But I had paid 5000 bucks to be here, so I had to have the ready-to-rock look.

'Yeah, man! Hurry up, we have to grab the last seats,' Karan said with immense excitement. He seemed like a kid going for his first school picnic.

Then Shanaya entered. As the boys eyes widened, their jaws dropped. She was wearing a black tank top and blue denim shorts. A pendant around her neck and two giant bangles on her wrist were her only accessories.

'Oh fuck! She has a tattoo on her back! Look! Look!' Karan whispered in my ears as she hugged Sunaina. As he insisted, I looked at her. She was definitely hot. I was getting turned on. I tried to look away, but she came up to me.

'Hi, Aarav,' she said and leaned forward to hug me. Before I could think of anything else, we had already shared half a half.

She then held my hand and said, 'Let's go, guys.'

What was happening? I asked myself, while the other three shared wicked smiles. Aniket winked at me as I gently let go of Shanaya's hand. For the guys at school, it was an honour to even have a word with Shanaya, and here I was, letting go of her hand.

The five of us headed towards our bus. Rahul and Oshit too accompanied us.

'Oh-shit!' we all called out in chorus and chuckled, while he gave a sheepish look. They were nice guys and were an important part of our group.

We entered our bus. Rahul had already grabbed the last seat with Oshit and Karan. It was obvious that the lovebirds Aniket and Sunaina would sit beside each other.

Shanaya sat alone in the seat behind Aniket and Sunaina, and looked like she wanted me to sit with her. To avoid any awkward situation, I took my place beside an unoccupied seat, plugged in my earphones, and looked outside the window. By now, everyone had pulled out their iPods, while Oshit took out his old-fashioned Walkman.

I leaned my head against the window and looked at the falling leaves outside. It was a bright sunny day. Aniket and Sunaina were already lost in each other, while those at the back started hooting.

All of a sudden, a kid entered the bus and sat alongside Shanaya. It seemed like he couldn't believe his good luck. Suddenly, a car stopped in front of the bus, and everyone, except me, got up wondering who it was.

But my disinterest turned into interest when Sunaina's scream pierced through my ear plugs, 'Oh! Here she is!'

'Oh my, my! It is Anamika Roy.' I heard someone say. My heart skipped a beat. And when I saw her, I was breathless. Anamika Roy! She was here!

Her untied hair hid half her face. She looked a bit confused. She was busy finding something in her handbag standing right next to the door of the bus. Oh, she looked so pretty in her purple spaghetti top and cargo shorts!

I could not take my eyes off her. All I wanted now was to see her full face.

My iPod seemed like it had a mind of its own, and in total sync with mine. It started playing Jay Sean's 'Got My Eyes on You' as soon as I saw her.

The tour manager closed the door.

In the next ten seconds, she was standing beside me, greeting Sunaina and Shanaya. I combed my hair with my fingers, wiped the sweat off my face, and slyly sniffed my armpits to check if I was stinking.

The most amazing thing was that in the whole bus I was the only one sitting alone, and it was a sixteen-hour journey. I was super excited! But soon, doubt took over. What if she sat at the back making someone else sit with me instead? What if she convinced the 'lucky kid' sitting with Shanaya to join me; or worse, what if she declared in front of everyone that she did not want to sit with me!

Then I plugged my earphones back with some attitude. I had heard it said that if you are crazy about a girl, you should never show it overtly. The best thing to do is to wait for a while, throw some attitude and let her approach you. At the same time, I also started wondering if that could be the reason why I had been single for so many years.

However, such things are easier said than done. I could not help but steal glances at her. Yet, I tried to pretend that I was busy doing my own thing—while I had switched off my media player, I kept the earphones plugged in.

'Yaar, you sit here with Aarav, we will keep swapping after some time. We are anyway almost sitting together, na,' Sunaina told Anamika, while she nodded. My heart started beating fast.

'Hi,' Anamika said, suddenly turning towards me, but she was not smiling. Unfortunately, I was again sniffing my armpits when she addressed me. A bad start indeed.

Immediately, I turned my head towards the window, as if to ignore her. This was out of sheer panic.

'Excuse me?' she said and left in a huff. I hated myself at that moment. She went straight to Shanaya and somehow convinced the kid to join me. My fake stud-like attitude had failed miserably.

I was crestfallen. The boy came to me with a PlayStation in his hands and a packet of chips.

'I want the window seat,' he ordered. He was barely four feet in height and probably twelve years old. 'What? What did you just say?' I questioned in a way that would terrify him.

'Are you deaf or what? I think the girl was right,' he said, as my eyes widened.

'Girl? What did she say, which girl?'

'Yes, that girl in purple. She said you were dumb and deaf. I gather now that she was right.' He pointed towards Anamika. My eyes widened even more.

There you go! Now show your pathetic attitude, you sucker, I said to myself.

I told the kid to take the aisle seat for a few hours and shut the fuck up. He sat next to me, playing some stupid game and munching on the chips very loudly. I started my media player again, this time switching to Pankaj Udas, his surname reflecting my state of mind.

Half an hour passed. Aniket and Sunaina were in the same cuddling position. My classmates in the last row were busy yelling.

Shanaya and Anamika were busy gossiping, while the kid still munched on his chips blissfully without even bothering to offer me any.

'Why do you keep staring at that girl? Is it because she has really sexy legs?' He suddenly asked, leaving me in a state of shock. How could a kid talk like that?

'What? Are you nuts? Should I tell your teacher you said this?' I tried to scare him.

'Should I tell that girl now?' he asked and stood up. I pulled him down and apologized.

'Please calm down, son,' I said.

'Okay, then tell me the truth,' he said.

'Okay, okay! See, I'm not looking at her. Actually, I'm looking at the girl sitting next to her,' I explained.

'The purple one?'

'Yeah, the purple one.'

'But she doesn't have sexy legs like the black one,' he said. *This kid must have already entered puberty*, I concluded. He was looking at Shanaya more intently than anyone else.

'Look, kid, I'm not looking at anyone's legs. I am looking at the purple one,' I maintained.

'But why? Do you like her?'

'Don't you think you are asking too many questions, kid?'

'Don't you want to sit with her?' said the smart-arse.

'Can you help me with that?' I asked, raising my left eyebrow.

'If you want me to!'

'Okay then, let that be the case,' I said.

'But . . .' he smiled wickedly.

'What but?' I asked with both my eyebrows raised this time.

'You have to introduce me to that girl in black.'

'Have you hit puberty, kid? It sounds like you have a crush on her.' I laughed.

'Dude, I whack off three times a day, so better shut up!'

'What the hell!' I was stunned.

'Not hell, it feels like heaven! Aahh . . .' This made me laugh.

'Okay, okay, I'll do that for you. But what will you do after I introduce you to her?' I was still unable to control my laughter.

'Leave the rest to me,' he said confidently.

He went straight to the girls. I was nervous. What was he going to do?

He murmured something folding his hands, as if he was pleading. No matter what, I wanted Anamika. I saw her stand up and the kid take her seat. Oh my god! Fifteen hours straight with Anamika! A shiver ran through my body seeing her approach me.

Super Kid, that's what I shall call him from now on.

I welcomed Anamika with a smile. She did not return the smile, but quietly sat down beside me.

'Ahem, ahem,' I cleared my throat. It worked. She looked at me; her face was still expressionless. I looked at her from the corner of my eye. She opened her bag and pulled out certain things. A comb came out first, then gloss, and finally, chewing gum.

'Do you want to have one?' she asked all of a sudden. I was taken aback.

'No thanks, I mean thank you.' My voice choked. She started combing her hair, almost leaning on me, her body tilted in a way that her bare shoulders were brushing against mine. I tried to make some space between us, and I succeeded. What was that now? The girl I dreamt of was just inches away from me, almost leaning on me, and I pulled back? What the heck? What was wrong with me?

'Oh, sorry . . . I was just . . .' she apologized.

'It's okay,' I said with a smile. Her face still did not reflect any emotions. And I was not one of those flirtatious lads who could get girls to smile at the drop of a hat.

We sat quietly for the next few minutes. I saw that Super Kid was busy feeling up Shanaya. His hand was on her bare left leg. Lucky, horny chap! I should have perhaps taken some tips from the kid instead of sitting here like a loser.

It was 7.30 p.m. now. It had been an hour and all that we had exchanged was a sorry and a thank you. The kid, on the other hand, had shamelessly touched Shanaya's entire body in the past one hour. I regretted my childhood—it had been spent playing with cars and useless toys.

We now reached Haveli on GT Karnal Road. A buffet had been organized for us. There was a lot of yawning and stretching as we stepped out. It was extremely pleasant outside. Anamika covered herself with a black stole. Everyone moved towards the garden area for dinner. Some went to the washroom, while others went to smoke. Aniket and Sunaina went for the swings in the lawn. There was a slight breeze, it was perfect weather for paramours.

Soon everyone started queuing up with dinner plates. The food made my mouth water. I joined Karan, Oshit and Rahul in the queue.

I looked around for Anamika, but couldn't spot her. The main course was followed by dessert.

As for Aniket and Sunaina, they were not bothered about food at all.

'Hey, Aarav, come, let's gather everyone. We'll all sit together here on the grass,' Karan shouted.

'Okay, you try and disturb Aniket and Sunaina. I'll be back in a moment,' I said.

'But where are you going?' he asked.

I showed him my little finger, gesturing that I was going to pee. I went through the garden area, crossing the ice cream parlour. I was moving towards the washroom, when I saw a familiar girl sitting alone on a table for four.

It was Anamika. The place was in the midst of bushes, minimally lit up. I assumed that it was specially made for lovers, but she was the only one sitting there. I headed towards her, forgetting all about the washroom. Probably not the best idea.

'Hey, Anamika, what brought you here, dear? Come, let's join the group. Did you have dinner?' I wondered where the words came from.

'No, it's okay, you go. I'll stay here,' she said as she wiped off tears from her eyes. I went closer.

What was the matter? Have I done something stupid? Why was she crying? I asked myself.

'Hey, what happened? Why are you crying?' I anxiously asked her. Then I added, 'Missing mummy, huh?'

But it was all in vain, perhaps because of the lame talk about mummy.

'No, nothing like that. You go, don't spoil your moment,' she said in a sweet, quivering voice, wiping off another tear.

It destroyed my soul to see her cry. This seemed like a serious matter. Should I interfere?

'Well, I won't intervene in this against your will. All I want to say is that crying is not the solution to any problem. You can figure out the solution easily with the help of your beautiful smile.' I myself broke into a smile and felt pleased at my first attempt at flirting.

She looked at me with tears in her eyes and finally forced a smile on her innocent little face. 'Thanks, Aarav, this really means a lot to me,' she said with a genuine smile that lit up her face. I was lost in the beauty of her eyes.

'See, dumb and deaf people can make you smile too,' I said with a half-smile and she broke into spontaneous laughter.

'Can make you laugh too, apparently.'

'Oh, I'm really sorry about that, Aarav. Please don't mind.' Once again she smiled, this time at her prettiest.

'It's okay, no grudges at all, it happens,' I said casually. 'So, shall we go now?'

'Sorry, but I'm in no mood to join anyone now. You please go, Aarav. I'm really okay here.' She was once again glum.

'By the way, did that kid say something about me?'

'Yep, he told me that you're a child abuser.'

'What, me? Child abuser?' My jaw dropped.

'And a porn hoarder too! He said you'd wreck his mind by your dirty talk, and so he needed to shift to some other place. He almost begged.' My face had turned red.

'But I don't think so. You look so innocent.' She tried to put me at ease.

'He's a liar, Anamika. I haven't watched a single porn movie in my entire eighteen years. What exactly is a porn movie, by the way?' I asked. Surely, I was overdoing this.

She laughed hard and said, 'Don't overdo it, Aarav!'

'He did that just because he wanted to sit with Shanaya, and I wanted . . .' I stopped.

'What did you want?' she asked, the question looming in her eyes too.

I felt a lump in my throat. 'I wanted him to leave if he wanted to. So he used me, I guess. Such a horny kid.' I couldn't bring myself to tell her the truth.

'He said you're horny too,' she said, sticking out her tongue.

'He's such an ass,' I said.

'Hey, he's just a kid! Leave it. I know you're not like that.' Once again, she gave me that smile that could melt hearts. I was totally flattered. I liked it that she had not got me wrong.

We fell quiet for a while. Then she broke the silence.

'You know what? You're really dumb.' She smiled once again.

'But why?' I smiled too, but in shock.

'A girl is sitting all alone with you, the weather is so pleasant, no one is around and yet you haven't even asked me what I would like to have.'

I was overjoyed. I rushed to the counter and ordered two cappuccinos.

'Now?' I asked as I sipped the coffee.

'Hmm, the coffee is good.' She smiled, taking a sip.

'I'm talking about me being dumb, Anamika.' As I said that, I was looking intently at her cute little moustache made by the creamy cappuccino.

'You're not dumb any more. The coffee is good.' She now broke into a good-natured laugh.

We sipped our coffees looking at the bushes, sharing smiles every other moment. Time passed in smiles.

'Oh! Oh! Something fishy going on?' Sunaina screamed all of a sudden from behind the bushes. Before we could recover, Aniket, Karan, Oshit, Rahul, Shanaya and even the kid joined in and started hooting. I looked at Anamika. She was laughing.

I was relieved and started laughing. But when I locked my eyes with the kid, I gave him a dirty look. He just winked and smiled. This kid was way too smart.

'Nothing like that, guys,' Anamika tried to clear the air.

'Guys, shut up! I think we should leave, we're getting late.' I started walking towards the bus; everyone followed, giggling.

'Going great, sir!' the kid said as he elbowed me in the rib and ran to Shanaya.

We were in the bus again. Fourteen more hours with Anamika! Heaven!

She asked for the window seat and I complied without any hesitation. We headed towards our final destination—Manali. All the windows of the bus were wide open. Chilly breeze was flowing all around, ruffling our hair. Oshit started playing some old Kishore Kumar tracks, making the ambience all the more lovely: '*Dil kya karey, jab kisi ko kisi se pyaar ho jaaye', 'Ek ajnabi haseena se yu mulaqaat ho gayi.'* I secretly thanked Oshit. *Oshit, you're no longer Oh-shit!*

But one question still burdened my heart: Why was Anamika crying? I wanted to know, but I dared not ask her. I did not want her to stop smiling.

Anamika was gazing outside the window. In her black stole, spectacles in her hand, and her hair tied tight, but with a few strands swinging over her face due to the wind. I wanted to tuck them behind her ears. Would she like that or would she think it was too much of a liberty? Confused, I dropped the idea.

She closed her twinkling eyes for a while. I just looked at her, pretending as if I was looking outside. I could not take my eyes off of her. People might think I was ogling at her, I say it was a rare bond between my eyes and her beauty.

Hours passed by, she kept sleeping in the same posture. I looked across for a moment. Everybody was asleep. Even Aniket and Sunaina, holding hands, with Sunaina resting her head on Aniket's shoulder in that romantic way. Sounds of loud snoring could be heard from the back. It was 11.30 p.m. by my watch. I decided to close my eyes too.

I heard someone sobbing. I opened my eyes and looked around. It was Anamika. Her eyes were still closed, but tears were rolling down her cheeks. She was shivering.

'Hey, Anamika, what happened? Please don't cry,' I tried to console her. But I've never been good at consoling. Her sobs became louder.

I thought of wiping off those falling pearls from her eyes. I dropped the idea quickly!

I had no idea what to do. I asked stupidly, 'Is something wrong?'

But she ignored my question and continued weeping.

'Please don't cry,' my voice almost broke.

She finally looked at me. Perhaps I looked funny. I don't care, but at least it brought a sudden smile on her face, if only for a fraction of a second.

'I'll be fine,' she said as she tried to smile; at the same time a tear dropped again from her glittering eyes. She wiped her tears with her handkerchief.

Suddenly, she held my hand and closed her eyes again. Now this was something beyond special. No shiver went through my body this time; no beads of sweat covered my body. It is possible that it was because my body was completely paralysed and my senses were numb. I felt nothing, and my heart forgot to skip beats.

I held her hand tightly. There was a perfect silence around us. I remembered when I had seen her for the first time, a year ago, and she was as beautiful now as she was then. I tried to sleep but her hand was still held firmly in mine. Now our hands were getting sweaty, so it was time to disconnect.

Dutch Courage

We reached Manali the next morning. Karan woke me up. I looked around, all the seats were empty. I wondered if Anamika was fine by now.

We took our luggage and headed towards the hotel. Karan, Aniket and I were to share the same room.

'Oh my goodness! Look at that! What a view!' Karan shouted as we entered our hotel room. I stepped forward to accompany Karan at the window.

The snow-covered mountains cast a shadow over the little town. The dim sunlight sparkled against the peaks. The evergreen conifer trees swayed in the cool breeze. Narrow roads paved their way through the mountains like a snake. The mountains seemed to be touching the sky.

I was rendered speechless by the beauty in front of me. I closed my eyes to lock it up in my mind. Karan started clicking pictures. I felt too peaceful to jump for photographs, so I simply claimed a corner of the bed and lay down.

Aniket's phone buzzed. Sunaina informed him that she was sharing a room with Shanaya and Anamika.

The three of us decided to rest for a while.

It was 3.00 p.m. when someone knocked at our door, forcing us to get up.

'Who the fuck is that?' Aniket moaned in deep slumber. The knock continued as we decided to ignore it. Nobody was ready to stand up and open the door. We pushed Karan off the bed and he had no choice but to open the door.

'Anamika,' he said. I got up in haste, probably the quickest I have ever gotten up in my entire life. The reflex was so quick that I could not even sense that I had stepped on Aniket's face until he accused me of it. I paid no heed to the mutt and got off the bed to meet her.

'Hi,' she said.

Karan patted my back and hid behind the door.

'Hi,' I replied with a smile. 'How are you now? Umm . . . what happened?'

'I'm good. Just came to see you,' she said. I was delighted. What? See me? Me? I asked myself before asking her the same.

'Everyone else is pretty occupied with something or the other, and err . . . I needed someone who would listen to me,' she said as Karan giggled from behind the door.

'Oh sorry . . . I mean . . . ya sure,' I said as I moved out, closing the door behind me quickly.

'I think it would have been better if you'd come out in something decent,' she said.

'What?' I asked, shaking my head in confusion.

'Actually, your boxers look quite funny, with this Mickey Mouse stuff on it,' she said as I looked down. In the confusion, I had forgotten to put on my jeans—truly embarrassing!

We both chuckled as I left to change.

We walked down the banks of Beas River, which flows across the Kullu–Manali hills.

We went down the rocky plains, close to the roaring river. Anamika's hair danced in the wind. We walked, admiring the beauty around us.

'So? Why are we here? Is there anything important you want to talk about?' I asked, wondering if I sounded rude. I almost expected her to begin her reply with her most used phrase: 'nothing like that'.

'No, nothing like that,' she began. I congratulated myself for getting it right.

'I just wanted to say sorry to you for yesterday. I was literally exhausted. So, I uttered whatever came to my mind. I should not have bothered you with my problems. And then I didn't even tell you the reason. I just can't share it, hope you won't mind. I am so sorry for being a pest last night. I'm so, so sorry,' she said, looking down.

'No, no, nothing like that,' I laughed.

'Shut up!' she said.

'Well, I don't think I was *bothered.*' I stressed on the word. 'In fact, I was extremely pleased that I could be of use to anyone on this planet.' I gave her a smile and she grinned.

We stood facing each other now. I looked straight into her eyes, which reflected the fascinating smile on her face.

'I'd always love to help you out, Anamika. Whether you want me to or not, I will be there.' I didn't know where I got the strength to put it that way, but I said it straight to her face.

'You know what?' she said, looking at me while I stared at her pink slippers. I was very apprehensive about her response.

'What?' I said in a low tone.

'You're just so good. It feels extremely good to be with you. Despite the fact that we are not close, the ease with which you helped me is commendable. I am really thankful to you.' I sighed in relief.

'I guess these are moments that turn strangers into good friends.' I was learning to talk more freely now. I had learnt it all by myself.

'Friends?' she asked as we shook hands. It was all rather movie-like.

'Friends,' we uttered in unison and chuckled. Our laughter echoed across the river. Our fifteen-minute walk ended before we knew it. It was ended by Sunaina calling Anamika for lunch on her cellphone.

After lunch, we changed and left for Van Vihar for rafting. Anamika and I did not interact much after that walk except for some quick little smiles and fleeting eye contacts. I would glance at her every five seconds and then she too would be looking at me. This made me confident.

But when it was time for dinner, again, the interactions were brief: 'Would you like to have this?' 'Can you pass me that ?' 'Can you please move a bit?' 'Excuse me.'

'Hey, what's the scene for tonight, man?' Karan asked as Aniket joined us. Rahul and Oshit were busy with some personal issue, while Shanaya, Sunaina and Anamika were in the middle of some conversation.

'What scene?' I asked.

'It includes huge quantities of booze,' Aniket winked.

'What? You know I don't drink,' I protested.

'C'mon, man, you're a grown-up now. Nobody is here to bother you. No parents, nothing. Just gulp down some shots, tiger,' he tried to persuade me.

'Okay, but not today. Today is a Tuesday and I can't start with this thing on a Tuesday.'

They both laughed.

Bloody atheists!

'Okay then, tomorrow it is,' Aniket said as we walked towards the hotel. Our hotel was not very far from Mall Road where we had our dinner. Aniket and Sunaina were walking hand in hand ahead of us, while Shanaya and

Anamika were talking to each other, constantly smiling. We reached our rooms and changed into pajamas. At 11:30 p.m. the phone in our room rang.

'Hello,' Aniket said as I was preparing to lie down on the bed. 'Anamika, okay!' I jumped up soon as I heard him take that name.

'She wants to talk to you,' Aniket said and gave me the phone.

'What's going on, boss?' Karan inquired, jokingly.

I showed them the middle finger and signalled to them to stay away from my business.

'Hello,' I said, clearing my throat.

'Hello! Ahem! Ahem!' Karan imitated and kicked my butt.

'Hello,' Anamika said meekly.

'Yes, what happened?' I asked.

'No, nothing like that. I just wanted to say goodnight,' she said in the sweetest voice possible.

I laughed slightly. 'What? That's it?'

'What more were you expecting?' she asked as she laughed and hung up without even waiting for my reply. I could hear Shanaya's and Sunaina's chuckles in the background. It took me a minute to get over the incident, when a thought entered my little brain: *Had I just been prank called?* I wondered who it could have been. I was confused, but then the phone rang again. I picked it up.

'I love you,' a feminine voice said, throwing me into a state of surprise and confusion.

'What?' I screamed as my heartbeat increased at an exponential rate.

'Aniket?' she asked.

'Sunaina?' I asked. Phew!

'Aarav?' she asked.

I laughed.

'Oh, sorry! I thought it was Aniket. I'm really sorry, don't tell anyone. Can you just . . .' Sunaina pleaded in an embarrassed tone.

'Yeah sure, don't worry,' I said, controlling my laughter.

'Love is calling you, *jaanu*,' I said to Aniket, kicking his butt. Karan and I couldn't stop laughing. Soon after that, I became preoccupied with my thoughts once again. The thought that it had been Anamika numbed my heart.

Aniket and Sunaina ended up talking the entire night. Karan and I had to cover our ears with pillows to avoid those sweet nothings.

* * *

I didn't know when I fell asleep, but one thing I was sure of—I slept thinking of Anamika. The second day started with another knock on the door and as usual, no one was interested in opening the door. 'Get up or else we will leave without you for Rohtang Pass,' a hoarse male voice declared.

All of us stood up like army cadets. I had never imagined that we would ever fight to take bath before the others, but that's what we did. After a lot of commotion, we were ready! Glasses, watches, shoes and deodorants—we were well equipped for the trip.

The day passed in Rohtang Valley clicking photographs, eating lunch and sightseeing, but all the while I could not spend time with Anamika. Moreover, no eye contact, no smiles, nothing. I had no conversation with Anamika that day. It was a bad day for me.

'What about beer today?' Aniket asked, in a state of exhilaration.

'What?' Oshit and I asked in chorus.

'You are all grown-ups. It is now or never!' he said, trying to convince us.

'But I haven't tried anything like this before. What if I pass out?' I asked in an innocent tone.

'*Saale, mai kya yaha bewda baitha hu*? We are all first-timers, man! Let's celebrate this moment of life. It will *not* come again.' Aniket was at his manipulative best.

Finally, we gave in.

Oshit, Rahul and I stayed back in the hotel, while Karan and Aniket were given the responsibility of smuggling in the booze. The three of us sat on the entrance stairs waiting for them. I was getting paranoid. What if a teacher caught us drinking? What if we created a scene after drinking? What if I went to town about Anamika? What if I proposed to her after drinking?

The rest of them were at the bonfire. Earlier, I had seen Anamika laughing as sparks of flame soared in the air. She was looking stunning in a deep-neck top—with red, white and black stripes—and denim shorts. She was not wearing her glasses. Her brown eyes were glowing like pearls.

Sunaina asked me about Aniket's whereabouts. I told her that I had no idea. Our heartbeats increased as people started asking about the missing duo.

'What should we do, Aarav? I have an intuition that we will get caught and be sent back to Delhi tonight after they inform our parents about this!' I froze at the dire prospect.

Then I made up my mind and commanded, 'Let's go and stop them.'

We headed towards Mall Road from the back of the hotel. We ran into them at the end of the road.

'Look what I've got!' Aniket said with a wicked smile on his face.

'We aren't doing this, Aniket,' I said, gathering some strength to snatch the bag full of beer cans and a whisky bottle.

'Are you nuts?' Aniket yelled, throwing his hands up.

'What if a teacher catches us drinking? What if we create a scene after getting drunk? What if I force . . .' I stopped myself as I realized what I was going to say.

'Force?' Karan asked.

I bit my tongue and tried to stay calm.

'We are not doing this. That's it,' I said as Aniket and Karan snatched the bag from my hand. They took out a can of Foster's and gulped it down in one go.

'What the hell?' Rahul finally broke his silence. Oshit stood silently in panic. 'Ahhh, this is life!' Aniket said as we made a face. Karan opened the whisky bottle as Aniket's phone rang.

'Yeah, baby, we will be back in five minutes for sure,' he said. It must be Sunaina.

'Who was that?' Oshit asked, looking really terrified.

'Anamika,' Aniket whispered. Foster's was doing its job on him.

'What did she say?' I asked.

'She said she loves you, asshole,' he slurred.

'Just shut the fuck up, Aniket, you're drunk! Let's get back to the hotel,' I declared.

'Do you think I'm kidding? Why don't you go and ask her? And if you don't have the guts, whisky will surely help you,' he said as everyone laughed at me.

'C'mon, Aarav, now or never!' exclaimed Karan as I gave it a second thought and snatched the bottle from his hand. I smelled it. It smelled exactly like cough syrup to me. I was still a kid.

'Go on, she'll be off to bed soon,' Aniket provoked me again. As I took a sip, I felt like vomiting, but Karan pushed my head back and helped me swallow the alcohol. It was the first time in my life and it was good though.

I gulped some pegs neat on an empty stomach and in a hurry. I felt both warm and cool at the same time.

We reached the hotel somehow. The bonfire party was over. Aniket, Karan and I were almost out of our senses. Aniket yelled gibberish, while Karan kept laughing without any reason. I was looking for Anamika.

'C'mon, boy,' Aniket said as he patted my shoulder. He was winning—I was doing what he wanted me to. So this was what people meant when they talked about peer pressure.

When we finally met Anamika, all of us decided to go down to the river. I could barely move and for the life of me, I don't know how I managed to reach there without falling.

'Hi, sweetheart,' I said and smiled when I finally got Anamika beside me.

She gave me that what-did-you-just-say look.

I stepped forward towards her, and the next thing I felt was the ground.

'Where are you, Anamika? I want to say something.'

'Hey, Aarav, are you all right? Get up, I am here,' she expressed deep concern.

'Hey, Anamika, I am so glad to see you again. I am fine,' I chuckled.

'Aarav, are you drunk?' she asked in a raised tone, looking away.

'Shh! All this is for you.' I looked straight into her shining brown eyes. There was silence all around.

'What's happening here? Will someone please explain?' she panicked.

I managed to stand up straight on my own. I stepped forward to take her hand into mine and went on my knees. Karan hooted and laughed. His voice echoed and disturbed me. I took out the first thing that I came across in my pocket and threw it at Karan. It hit Rahul instead but my aim was achieved. Silence spread all over.

I got back to Anamika. Her soft hands were cold, yet sweaty. I began.

'I still remember the day I saw you for the first time. The moment I saw you, my heart went insane. I never had the guts to talk to you, never had the confidence to say "hi". I don't know what you do to me. I can't explain how you make me feel.'

I crawled closer to her, and gently rubbed her hand. She seemed to have frozen, and could come up with no response.

I breathed and continued.

'Anamika, you are the best thing that has ever happened to me. I love you . . .'

I waited for her to respond. She didn't even blink once. I felt dizzier with every passing moment.

I waited for her to say something, but darkness spread over her beautiful face. I felt as if I was floating in the air.

* * *

I don't know where I slept that night, and who dragged me to where I found myself in the morning. I'm not even sure if Anamika had slapped me or extended the courtesy of a rude refusal, bidding farewell to our newly built friendship as well.

I opened my eyes slowly, my mouth was stinking. One of Karan's heavy legs was on my stomach and the other between my legs. I got up, pushing Karan away. I took two baby steps and stumbled on Aniket, almost kissing him in the process. He woke up, alarmed and screamed with both hands on his chest, 'Don't rape me!'

But I ignored it, because all I cared about at that moment was Anamika. 'Shut the fuck up and tell me what happened.' I shook Aniket.

'What, what happened? I don't know. I have not done anything! God knows that I am loyal to Sunaina,' he said.

'Oh, just shut up! What did I do last night?' I looked at him with hopeful eyes.

'I think . . . well, I don't know. I just know that Rahul brought me here.'

Aniket's uncertain replies made my heart sink. I went to the washroom in utter dejection and got ready for the day. Then it struck me that it would probably be wise to call Sunaina if I wanted to know more about what had happened last night. I hurriedly took a bath and came out.

I dialled 76 and waited anxiously.

'Hello,' Anamika's sweet voice greeted me.

I trembled. In a shivering voice, I replied to her, 'Hello, Anamika?'

A long silence hovered between us until I heard a click! She had hung up!

What should I do now? I had infinite questions boggling my mind, but not a single answer. I sat down like Devdas, not drunk this time.

'We are leaving the hotel in five minutes,' Rahul peeped inside the room and informed.

I carelessly packed my bag and gave a dirty look to anyone who was trying to talk to me.

I stepped down the stairs and approached the bus. I was one of those who had arrived late and was thus greeted by ugly stares from those had reached on time. Everyone seemed depressed. The trip was over. I could not find Anamika in the bus. As I moved forward to sit alongside Karan, I saw Anamika looking outside the window of the last seat. She didn't even look at me. This meant I had messed it up big time. I sighed and sat with Karan, who was pretty busy with his iPod.

The journey back to Delhi was a monotonous affair until we stopped at Manikaran Gurudwara. A beautiful place with its hot water spring and spiritual essence, it instilled a sense of tranquillity in me. I was too scared to approach Anamika to clarify about anything. Everyone was pretty anxious to eat something from the *langar* pandal. I wasn't hungry. I was in love, I was scared, and I had messed it up.

I walked to the bridge over the hot-water spring. It was a makeshift wooden bridge. The view was mesmerizing. The river was silvery and wild.

'Aarav!' Out of the blue came Anamika's saccharine voice. I had no courage to look into her eyes, but I had no self-control as well. I turned and met her gaze. Her head was covered with a black scarf.

'Can we talk?' she asked, shrugging her shoulders like an innocent three-year-old.

I simply nodded. She sat beside me with a leaf bowl full of halwa.

'You seem to have lost your appetite, huh?' she began.

'Umm . . . nothing like that, just not hungry.'

'You're such a copycat,' She accused me.

'Anamika, I am so sorry about whatever . . .' I stopped midway as she pressed my hand gently.

'Aarav, I just want to say that I respect your feelings a lot but . . . umm . . . Well, I don't know why I like spending time with you. I love to talk to you. I feel so comfortable with you. I can trust you with my life. You are perhaps the only friend I can be with, always.' She spoke every word clearly and slowly.

So she likes me. I couldn't resist smiling.

'But this might not be possible. Destiny is not in my favour, Aarav. Having feelings for you is impulsive. I can't help it . . . but it's not me that I am concerned about.' She paused and looked straight into my eyes.

'You may regret having those feelings for me.' She winced and left before I could make sense of her words.

Love in Delhi

We boarded the bus for the last leg of our journey. Anamika had now decided to be my seat partner again. She left me in a clueless state. I could not start any conversation. I just sat beside her with a half-smile and raised eyebrows. My mind was blank and my body was numb. I looked somewhere in the air. There was an uncomfortable silence between us, at least from my side it was uncomfortable. She turned towards me. We made awkward eye contact, so I turned back. She giggled. Oshit filled the silence with some wonderful tracks.

Everyone was seated comfortably. I adjusted myself in my seat and placed my hands on my thighs. Out of nowhere, Anamika's hands had claimed mine. An electric shock took control of my senses. Unlike me, she was bold enough to take the initiative. She closed her eyes.

I wondered what it would be like to entwine my fingers in hers. Would she protest? But I chose to try it this time. She hesitated for a second, but soon became stable. I sighed.

I pressed her hand gently as she looked at me and blushed. She gave me the most charming smile I had ever seen. She rested her head lightly on my shoulder.

I could not wish for anything more. I didn't want anything more.

We remained in that position for a long time. My shoulder felt heavier now. She had dozed off.

Her hand was still safe in mine. Thankfully, no one decided to take a peek at our corner. I rested my head lightly on her head and closed my eyes.

But a sudden brake woke us up from our reverie. I nearly banged my head against the front seat, but a soft hand saved me. Anamika smiled as I looked at her gratefully.

'So, you plan to not talk till we reach Delhi?' Anamika asked playfully.

'Umm, no, nothing like that . . .' I said, and instantly realized that her favourite phrase was fast becoming mine too. I bit my tongue. She chuckled.

'I just don't know what to talk about after what you said to me at Manikaran.' I made a face.

For a moment, her face turned weird, but she quickly switched back to her smile.

'So whose idea was it?' she asked suddenly.

'What? What are you talking about?' I asked as if I didn't know what she meant.

'Drinking! Who suggested it?'

I gave her an apologetic look and pointed at Aniket.

'I knew it! It couldn't have been your idea,' she said and beamed.

We started talking about random things. Knowing her interests and dislikes was the prime objective of the conversation. In no time, I started loving Sourav Ganguly, and Mamata Banerjee became my favourite politician. And fish would be my staple, probably. I wanted to know everything about her. I wanted her to share her every secret with me, and I wanted to share mine in turn. I wanted this girl to be with me always. I was in love, once and for all.

The journey back to Delhi seemed easier now that Anamika and I had started talking. Finally, we reached our destination. Though I was happy to be back in my own city, I was anxious about having to part with Anamika.

Delhi was hot as always. I had missed the climate, the pollution and the noise. I had also missed the hustle and bustle of city life. But when the bus stopped, I realized that I had already started missing Anamika.

It was time to say our goodbyes.

'Umm . . . I just wanted to . . . well . . . thank you for making my trip so amazing,' Anamika said, smiling at me.

I could do nothing but smile back.

'School is still closed for summer break. I was wondering how we can contact each other,' she said.

'Are you on Facebook?' I asked.

'No, I'm not interested in all these social networking sites. To be honest, I don't even have a PC at home.' She smiled broadly. I loved her genuineness. People like me would never confess that they didn't even have a cellphone.

'Okay, I'll call you then. What's your number?'

She quickly got a paper and wrote the number on it. 'Here it is,' she said and smiled.

'Now you give me yours. I'll call you up!' she said and I started looking for an excuse.

'Actually, my phone is with Mum these days. She is concerned about my studies,' I half lied.

Then her phone rang. '*Aami aschi, Maa, ohh tumi dariye acho darao,*' she said, blinking her lovely eyes and smiling continuously. At the same time, she held her hand out to me to bid goodbye. I took it in both hands, leaving my luggage on the floor. As she left, I could hear her say, '*Haan, Maa, aami phone raakhchi ebaar.*'

My gaze followed her until she disappeared. Suddenly, I felt all alone.

Soon after she left, I saw my dad waving from a distance.

I walked towards him dragging my luggage along. He hugged me so tightly it felt like I had just returned from war. In the car, I closed my eyes to gather all the beautiful moments I had lived in the past few days. While I was stretching my body, I heard a rustle in my pocket.

I realized it came from the most important piece of paper I've ever owned. I patted my pocket and smiled to myself.

* * *

Once we reached home, I went straight to my room for a nap. I was tired out of mind.

The whole time I slept, I dreamt of her. When I woke up, I was bubbling with energy. I had grown up a lot in the last five days: I had my first drink; for the first time, I proposed to a girl although in a drunken fit. I suddenly had an urge to listen to her voice.

I noticed mom's phone on the dining table. It was always used like a public phone, available to anyone, any time. Well, the coast was clear. No one was around. I had the number, and I had the craving to talk.

I took out the piece of paper—those digits were not merely numbers now. They were magic codes to unlock my sweetheart's heart.

I was sweating as I dialled the number. It was an easy number to remember, or maybe it was my state of mind. I wanted to remember it for a lifetime.

Instead of the standard ring, I heard a baby laugh.

Had she played a prank on me?

'Hello!'

'Huh? Hello, who's this?' I asked, even though I had immediately recognized Anamika's sugary voice.

'Aarav? Is that you? Can you hear me?'

I regained my senses and answered, 'Yes, Aarav this side, how are you?'

'Heaven knows how much I have waited for you to contact me,' she said.

'I am so sorry. I was sleeping', I said.

'Oh, anyway, this is your personal number, right? I'll save it right away.' A woman called her from the background.

'Got to go, ma calling. Take care.' And snap, she hung up.

My personal number?

Well, let it be then, I decided. Mom is mine, the phone is hers, so the phone is also mine. I saved Anamika's name as 'Fish' on 'my' phone.

I decided I would stay in the vicinity of the phone at all times. But of course, that was not possible. While I was thinking this through, the phone beeped. It was a text message from Anamika: *Lucky 2 hav u in my lyf <3*

How adorable! My heart leaped with joy and I immediately pressed the reply button and typed: *Trust me, I am luckier than you*

As soon as I pressed the send button, I heard mum's footsteps.

Oh holy crap! I am screwed! Meanwhile, another text beeped.

'Whose message is it? Are you texting someone?' Mom asked in a tone of suspicion. I quickly read the message: *Shoo shweeett of u . . .*

I deleted it immediately.

'N . . . N . . . Nothing, Ma, just a sauna slim-belt advertisement, for Vaibhavi, I am sure,' I said and laughed.

'So how was the trip? It was very rude of you to come and sleep like that last night. We had been missing you so much, but you clearly didn't,' she said as she moved to the kitchen.

I was worried about the texts. Should I have told Anamika that this was not my number? No, not at all! I should perhaps have a lock code on the phone. But how would I justify a secret lock code on mum's phone?

I put the phone on silent mode for the time being. There must be a solution, and I had to figure it out.

'Are you listening?' Mom raised her voice.

'Oh yeah, Mum! Sorry for last night. The trip was really nice. Manali is a beautiful place.'

'I know. Your dad and I went to Manali for our honeymoon. We began our lives there,' she said, blushing a little.

'And so have I,' I said instinctively.

'What?'

'Oh nothing, Mom, I was just saying that it was a wonderful experience.'

All I needed now was a message package in mom's phone and it had to happen without her knowing.

Since then, mom's phone stayed with me almost all the time.

My days began with a good morning message and ended with a good night message from Anamika. It became our daily routine.

It was not always easy to be near the phone and I often had to make the excuse of using the calculator or the alarm clock.

The holidays were about to get over. I had no idea of the whereabouts of my textbooks or notes. All I knew about was the calculator and the alarm clock.

So wots ur plan tomoro? Anamika inquired.

um . . . nthn as such, wat abt u?

I was wondrin if I cud meet u tomoro, if possi, even a few mins wud work

yeah! Y not! Where? Wen?

actually it's my bday 2mrw

oHH!! I shud have known dat! M so sorry! V'l meet 4 sure!

okay den, dilli haat tom sharp at 12.00, gunnyt, take care

So it was her birthday tomorrow.

I had to get out of the house at any cost.

I should plan a surprise to make her day special. I smiled at the thought and slept, dreaming of her.

First Date and an Empty Wallet

11.00 p.m. I had to be the first one to wish her. The thought made me anxious. The phone! How could I keep it? Claiming all rights over the phone was just not possible after ten. I needed to plan a late-night study session. But how would I justify a study session in these vacations? No one would believe me.

I had to calm down. I could simply say that I had a test the next day and needed the phone calculator. Simple.

11.45 a.m. It was time for me to call her now. I didn't want anyone else to wish her before I did.

I ensured that no one would barge into my room and that I would be alone for the next few minutes. Then I dialled the golden digits.

'Hello!' she said in a drowsy voice.

'Ahem! Sleeping?' I asked, feeling a little guilty for disturbing her sleep.

She chuckled. 'Actually, I was feeling exceptionally sleepy today. You called so early, I hope you know you have stolen other people's chances of wishing me first.'

'Yes, I wanted to be the first one.' I could visualize her beautiful smile right then.

'Oh no, Shanaya is calling. But let it be. She can wait.'

Now that brought a smile to my face.

'Three minutes to go!' I started the countdown.

'Yeah, yeah!'

'You are not very excited about your birthday, are you?' I asked.

'Well, not much. All my friends are busy, so no birthday celebrations for me. That is the one big disadvantage of having your birthday during the vacations.' She sighed.

'Anyway, happy birthday to you . . .' I started singing the birthday song to her.

'Thanks a lot, dear. Oh, I need to go. I am so sorry. Goodnight. Bye.'

And bang! She hung up. Why did she always disconnect in such haste? Anyway, I had managed to wish her before anyone else.

The screen lit up. A message from Fish: *Wana meet u 2mrw EVNIN . . . dnt rply nw . . . gunyt*

My 'late-night study' ended abruptly and I claimed my bed.

'What are you doing? Where are you going? Don't you have your IIT coaching today?' Vaibhavi threw a dozen questions at me as I was getting ready to meet Anamika for our first rendezvous after the school trip. Hardly a week was left for the school to reopen and the last year of our school life to begin. Thinking about it reminded me of when I saw Anamika for the first time. How drastically things have changed since then!

'I need to go out, today is Aniket's birthday,' I said as I ironed my black shirt. 'And I'm taking Mom's phone, so call me once or twice every minute like you always do.'

'Mom's phone? No coaching? I think I should talk to Dad about this. You don't seem serious about your IIT preparations,' she yelled at me. I ignored her completely and customized the phone settings—a loud ringtone and a flashy wallpaper to flaunt.

I smeared some hair gel and sprayed deodorant almost twenty times all over my body. I was getting ready as if it was the evening of my engagement. My sister kept staring at me, trying to understand what I was up to. She was witnessing a whole new side of me. Finally, I left home in great excitement. It was a mid-July afternoon, slightly hot and humid. It was cloudy too. I reached the metro station faster than usual, taking long steps and most of the while wiping the sweat off my brow. I checked 'my' mobile every other minute, and sniffed my underarms to recheck if I smelled good. I wiped my shoes against my denim over and over again, and checked my reflection in the glass door of the metro. I texted her that I had left for Dilli Haat. She didn't reply. I reached Netaji Subhash Place metro station in around forty minutes, repeatedly calling her, but all in vain. After some time, there was a message from Anamika: *call urgent!*

I called her.

'I'm so so sorry,' she said and immediately, my exhaustion disappeared, but I was also anxious. 'I was busy shopping with bhaiya. He's getting married this November.'

'Shopping? But we were supposed to meet today, and I have already reached. This is not done!' I said, struggling to remain calm.

'Oh no! It just slipped my mind in all the excitement. I'm really sorry. Okay, just wait for me. I'm at Connaught Place. Will catch you in approx fifty-nine minutes,' she said, laughing slightly.

WHAT! You expect me to stand here for one goddamn hour? I said to myself, but finally uttered in a calm voice, 'Okay, I'm waiting for you, come soon.'

'You're so sweet, Aarav.' She giggled and hung up. That giggle was enough to replenish my excitement of meeting her. The temperature was forty degrees Celsius, and I had to wait for her for one whole hour . . . well, fifty-nine minutes to be exact.

I sat on a bench in the shade of a tree at Dilli Haat's entrance with a handkerchief, and sipped Coke.

The deodorant's effect was already fading and the awful stench of sweat was taking over. I cursed myself for using the hair gel. It had started absorbing dust particles. Everything was getting ruined!

Finally, the phone rang, bringing back some energy in me. It was Anamika.

'Hey, where have you reached?' I inquired in a low voice.

'I'm almost there, just five minutes. Wait for me!' she said and hung up.

After a while, I saw Anamika approaching. She stood out among the Dilli Haat crowd. She was wearing a long brown top and a pair of cream-coloured shorts, perfectly complementing each other. Two big bangles adorned her wrists, apart from a wristwatch; there was a black anklet around her right leg, glorifying her grey stilettos. She was carrying a tiny handbag.

'Hey, I'm really very sorry. Am I really late?' she asked as I stood up.

'No, you came right on time. I just came early to see if this place was safe for the birthday princess,' I said in an attempt to fight my negative vibes and make things pleasant.

'Aww, I'm so sorryyyy. Please, please forgive me,' she pleaded in her sweetest voice, rendering me defenceless.

'Oh! It's okay, Anamika. Let's not spoil the day,' I said with a smile as I handed over a card to her.

'Happy birthday, dear!' I hugged her.

'Thank you so much, Aarav. Ok now, what's the plan?' she smiled.

'Well, we are going in. Wait, let me get the tickets,' I said, and went to the counter.

'Two tickets for adults.'

'Forty rupees,' the guy said in a heavy voice.

I took out my wallet and my heart skipped a beat. I saw nothing but a metro card in it. What the hell! No money in my wallet! That too on my first date ever! On her birthday! Though it was supposed to be her treat, what would she think of me now? I was wasting valuable time at the counter. In my hurry to reach here without anyone at home knowing, I had forgotten to take money. What a disaster!

The man behind the counter ordered me to get out of the way.

It's not that I'm not smart enough to tackle my problems; it's just that I ponder over them way longer than needed.

'Tickets?' she asked as she stretched her right hand towards me.

'Ummm, actually, Ana . . .' I stopped.

'What?'

'Actually, Mom just called and she wants me to get home urgently. I think we should leave!' I said all of this in a single breath.

'What? Are you serious? You know I forced my brother to bring an end to his engagement shopping and ran out of there to meet you, Aarav!' she yelled.

'But how can I . . .' I interrupted.

'You don't know how hard it is to . . .' she stopped and looked away.

'Hard to?' I asked, stepping to the side where she was looking.

She smiled and replied, 'You know it is not easy to stay away from you. I like being with you Aarav! Please don't go this early,' she said, making a cute face.

'What are you thinking about?' she asked, waving her hand in front of my face.

'Hmmmm . . . nothing, just . . . I . . .' Then I blurted out the truth to her.

'Are you insane? Let me clarify some things to you, Mr Aarav. I would be happier taking a walk with you than sitting in some posh café. I would be happier listening to your beautiful words than pinning my ears to songs played in a disc, so please calm down.'

'I'm really sorry, Anamika. I was disoriented the moment I knew I was not carrying any money. So shall we go for a walk now with an empty wallet?' I asked and smiled at her.

'Perhaps you forgot it's my birthday, so the treat is on me,' She said, winking at me. I smiled apologetically.

We decided to walk from the NSP metro station till the Rohini West station. But before that, I went to the back gate of Dilli Haat, where I approached a long-moustached security guard. In my attempt at playing hero, I asked him, 'Uncle, is this the way to go in?'

'No, boy, buy a ticket and try from the other gate. This area is for VIPs. Now go away!' he snapped.

'Okay.' I stepped back with an innocent face. But now the guard placed a hand on my shoulder and said, 'Boy, I heard you people talking. You can go in. But be careful of what you are doing. Stay within limits, boy!' He was making it seem as if we were about to make love right there. All along, Anamika was watching open-mouthed.

I had no money on me and here I was, entering through the VIP gate! Hail security uncle! Anamika couldn't stop smiling. Although she did have money, the real fun lay in such situations. I felt like I had finally done something good for her. A Sri Lankan carnival was on. The most exciting thing was that there were free game trials. We played all kinds of games, like throwing rings, shooting balloons, jackpot, etc. Even though we won nothing, we had quite a lot of fun. We also looked at menu cards just to sit together for a few minutes. We even danced to the Sri Lankan beats.

'It was awesome! I had the best time of my life with you, Aarav!' she smiled, and I could have died with joy.

'I don't have words to describe the time I have spent with you, Shona!' I said. Now where did the last word come from?

'Shona?' she exclaimed.

'No! Actually, I didn't mean that,' I said, taken aback.

'No! It was so sweet of you! Do you know what shona means in Bengali? It means sweetheart,' she winked.

I was impressed with myself. 'So, can I call you by this name from now on, Shona?' I asked and we both laughed. Finally, we decided to leave as it was getting late for both of us.

I wondered why mom or Vaibhavi had not called. Was everything okay with them?

We started walking. Suddenly, it started drizzling.

'You like rain?' she asked abruptly.

'Umm . . . not much.'

'Oh! That means you don't like it.'

'No, nothing like that. I have always wanted to get drenched with someone special.' Whoa! I was learning to talk to a girl. She smiled and turned pink.

'Oh okay, and how many special ones have you been with till now?' She giggled.

I stopped and stepped right in front of her. There was absolute silence for a few seconds. Our eyes shared an unbreakable bond. I gathered all my love for her and said, 'You are the one, the special one.'

She immediately looked away.

'What happened?' I asked, worried.

'Well, you became pretty serious, eh?' she stuck out her tongue and laughed. Seeing her innocent smile, I couldn't suppress my smile and began laughing with her.

We walked without stopping till Pitampura. The rain had started getting heavier. Our little fingers found each other every few seconds and the sensation that rushed through my body was unexplainable.

I had never felt like this before. It made me so jumpy that I clutched her hand more tightly and we jumped over the puddles madly. Our little fingers were now intertwined. We were thoroughly drenched. Her clothes were drenched and had started becoming transparent. She was aware of it as she tried to cover herself with her hands. Her top was completely glued to her skin and she was feeling uneasy. I tried to look away as much as possible, but men passing by ogled at her. I could feel my blood boiling.

'Come!' I said as I grabbed her wrist and took her under a tree. We looked into each other's eyes and she put her arms down. She stepped forward and I wrapped her in my arms. It was a rare moment and in that moment, I finally understood the laws of thermodynamics.

People were staring at us. The hug became tighter with time. She clutched my shirt and put her face on my shoulder. My hands automatically reached her waist.

It felt like no one was around. Meanwhile, something in my jeans distracted me.

It was my phone. We separated as I took the phone out in a hurry. It was wet. The screen was flashing nothing, but I could hear a strange noise. My mom's phone was a goner. I was fucked.

Life after Love

We said our goodbyes and left. I hinted at her that my phone was messed up and now communication would be difficult. Little did she know that by difficult I meant impossible.

I was scared to be home.

'Oh, Aarav! You are dripping wet! Go and change before you fall ill!' my mother exclaimed. I was sure her concern would soon turn into mad anger. I did not have the courage to tell her about her phone, so I quietly placed the corpse on the table. I received only a cold stare from her at that moment. She looked through me every time I was sitting in the way of something she needed. The rest of the days till school reopened passed in silence. Silence of the graveyard is the best phrase to describe the setting. This is how I spent the rest of the days of my vacation—with a dead phone, and a perpetual ashamed look on my face.

School reopened in a few days. I was relieved. I would get to meet Anamika again. Lost in anticipation, the moment I entered school, I went looking for her. Friends were hugging and celebrating their reunion just like last year. Only this time, I too was a part of it. A light tickle near my waist stirred me. Her chuckle brought my heart to a halt.

'How have you been, Mister Aarav?' she asked, looking at me with her smiling brown eyes.

'How do you expect me to be when you are not around?' I quipped.

She blushed.

'Well, we're getting late for our classes. We must leave. See you then,' she said as she took my hand and pressed it softly with both her hands. The bell for recess rang and all of us jumped out of our seats. Anamika came to our class, smiling at me, and went to where Sunaina and Shanaya were sitting.

'Let's reach the canteen before the growls of my stomach humiliate all of you.' Karan grabbed me and Aniket by the shoulder and we marched out of the room. I saw her gaze following me from the corner of my eyes. It made me feel good.

When we got back to class, Anamika was still there. She walked out as I walked in. She hooked her little finger into mine and murmured something that I couldn't understand. By then, the teacher had entered, giving her final command to settle down. I was physically there, but mentally I was in the adjacent room.

I could not concentrate on studies that day. When the final bell rang, I saw Anamika standing with Sunaina and Shanaya, busy in a conversation. We shared another loving look and a smile. How I loved those moments!

The institution where I went for coaching was not very far from the school and I used to get there walking. Anamika lived two blocks away from the school, so no school bus for her as well.

'Institute today?' She came to me.

I nodded in reply and smiled.

'I told Mum that I need to join an institute,' she said.

'Oh! Yes, you must join one. It is high time,' I said in a commanding voice.

She laughed. 'I know, idiot! And I am planning to join your institute. Is it good enough?' She asked and winked.

For me, going to the institute was a torture, but if she joined, it would be a pilgrimage. My daydreaming knew no boundaries. I hardly had any complaints about life any more.

Before I knew it, she had joined my batch. It happened almost instantly and I could not believe my luck.

We walked together to the institute whenever we had classes and to her house when we didn't. Our relationship was growing, but our romance was totally without telephonic conversations, goodnight and good morning messages. But whatever, I was content with what I had.

* * *

'There's a mock test on Sunday. Those who have prepared well in advance have nothing to fear. Those who score less than the standard score will have the privilege of inviting their parents to our institute for tea.' Our teacher dropped this bomb on us, eyeing me intensely. Lately, I had not been attentive in the classes. Self-study sessions too ended in daydreaming.

School was no less. Friends had started suspecting that something was keeping me distracted.

'Hi, Aaaaaarav!' Shanaya dramatically drawled in her fake accent.

'Oh! Hi,' I grinned.

'You seem pretty occupied these days. Is it school, studies, assignments, institute, long walks . . .' I was tongue-tied.

Sunaina joined her, 'Seems like Aarav has no time for friends any more.' Both of them chuckled at my embarrassed expression.

'Nothing like that, we are just friends,' I explained.

'Ahaan, nothing like that . . . I have heard that before.' Sunaina would not let me get away that easily.

'Who are just friends? We merely said that you don't talk to us much.' The guys too joined in the mockery. I had no option but to laugh with them. Since that day, it became a daily routine for my friends to tease me by her name. They would suddenly shout out her name and laugh at me when I turned to look back. Their pranks knew no bounds.

Days passed this way. Anamika and I were inseparable.

* * *

'I don't want to go!' she insisted as we reached the institute on a rainy evening.

'Where? Class?' I raised my eyebrows at her frivolity.

'Hmmmm . . .' she pursed her wet lips. A cool breeze blew off her hair from her face. She tied them back, clenching her clip in her lips. I could not take my eyes off her.

'Hello!' She brought me back to earth by waving her hand in front of my face.

'Oh! I was just thinking that skipping today's class isn't that bad an idea,' I smiled, adding, 'Your parents?'

'Mom and Dad come back after eight and bhaiya is not in town. So I have to be back by seven. Four hours to go!' Her eyes glittered.

'So what's the plan?' I asked.

'Ummm . . . you decide, I'll follow.' She took my breath away when she said that.

'Okay, India Gate?' I asked.

'Not bad, great weather too.' We sprinted towards the metro station.

In the train, we passed our time observing people and laughing at the eccentricities of some of them.

'It looks so beautiful!' she exclaimed as we gazed at India Gate, right in the heart of Delhi.

'Ice cream?' I asked.

'Wallet?' she mocked.

'Shut up, Shona! Not empty this time, tell me which one?'

'Black currant swirl.' I loved the way the ice cream gave her a cute little moustache. We giggled and talked about a lot of things. She played a few romantic songs on her cellphone, and they made us feel even more intimate.

'It's five, Aarav! I think we should leave now if we want to reach home by seven.'

'Hmm . . . let's go!' I said, munching on a chip.

'But we still have an hour, I guess. I mean, even if we leave by six, we will be able to reach home in time. Connaught Place?' I suggested and she smiled.

We walked around both the inner and outer circles of Connaught Place. Our fingers were intertwined all the way through.

'Your station is next, ' I said as I let go of her hand in the train.

'We still have two more minutes,' she held my hand again and I was only too willing.

We looked at each other for one last time for the day as she alighted.

That's how one of the best days of my life ended.

'Oh! Come in,' Vaibhavi said as she opened the door.

'You must be tired. How was your chemistry class?' she asked, stressing on chemistry. I was confused.

'Mom, give your child something to eat, he must be hungry,' she yelled.

'What happened, Vaibhavi? Do you want some favour?' I chuckled.

'Me, no! But you're soon going to ask me for one.' She flashed an evil smile.

'But you didn't answer. How was your class?' she asked again as mom came in.

'It was good! Learnt a few more things about chemistry,' I said sarcastically.

'For god's sake, stop lying, Aarav! There was no class today!' Mom said.

'And who told you that?' I mumbled.

'Your institute supervisor called to inform that there would be no class today. Now tell us where you were.'

'Came home straight, why?' I was nervous by now.

'Do you know my friend Sucheta?'

'That tall, filthy girl who can beat even you in gossiping? Yes, I know her.'

'Just shut up!'

'Why are you asking such random questions?'

'Let me tell you something that might interest you further. She lives near Connaught Place.'

That rocked me.

'How does this concern me? Look, I am really tired. I have to study a lot, so I should get back to it.'

'Aarav, you better concentrate on your studies rather than wasting your time on useless relationships.'

That was the body blow. Giving me a withering look, she handed me my plate the way one gives leftovers to a stray dog. She got back to her room, slamming the door behind her.

You cannot escape what life throws at you. You can't quit. You can't step back. You have to play the game until your last breath.

I went to bed thoroughly shaken.

It was 1.00 a.m. and the world was asleep. I looked around, discreetly took Vaibhavi's phone and changed the SIM. The phone was mine for the entire night now.

There were nine unread messages waiting for me. There were three from Anamika:

I'm missing you! :)

had a great day with you, do reply

okay don't reply back, Ignore me! Huh!

I texted her back: *u dere?*

I received her reply within seconds. She was awake!

Oh! Finally a message from you Mr Sharma

I typed 'I love you', but then changed it to a subtler 'I miss you'. As soon as I sent the message, I saw Vaibhavi coming out of her room.

I cleared the text and deleted the whole conversation in a hurry.

Soon, she went away after drinking water.

What happened? Anamika had messaged and she sounded restless.

I'm missing Manali. I wrote back.

but I'm missing someone more than Manali

Who? I knew, but I asked anyway, desperate to hear my name from her mouth.

shut up! You know she replied.

tell me nevertheless I teased her.

bhaiya is awake and mocking me, I'm going to sleep, felt good that you msgd atleast. Bad timing though!

Okay, gunnyt! Take care love you

I erased the last two words and messaged her the rest. I gazed at the mobile screen in anticipation of another message from her, but when it didn't come, I retired to bed.

I had no clue that Sunday, the day of the mock test, was near and I realized that it also meant that the tea party to which my parents were invited was also approaching.

I knew that I could not change my performance status in one day, and so I had renewed my faith in god. During the test, I marked the answers randomly on the OMR sheet and made hearts and cartoons of us to amuse myself. The results were to be out the very next day.

'Anamika Roy, kindly come forward,' the teacher announced as he picked up an answer sheet.

Oh lord, if he says anything to my girl, I am literally going to leave this institution. A bad score is no reason for humiliating an innocent girl like that. Marks are not the only criterion for assessment, I thought to myself.

Anamika got up and went to the front.

'You have topped the batch. Good job, girl. Keep it up!' Everyone clapped for her.

I laughed at myself for being so stupid.

'Aarav Sharma.'

So I had gotten the second highest marks. Well, not bad.

I walked confidently, appreciating my good luck.

'Do your parents like coffee or tea?'

'Sir?'

'You are one of the rare students who have scored a little more than zero in this test. Fortunately, you are the only one in this batch. Kindly tell your parents to come and meet me tomorrow. A call will be made to ensure that they do come, in case you *forget* to tell them about the same.'

Speechless, I went back to my seat; embarrassed, but mostly scared about the future.

The next day, dad came for 'tea'. The results were not at all what I wanted them to be. It saddened me to let down the only person in my family who believed in me blindly.

'You must pay attention to your studies now. It is a crucial stage, dear,' Anamika said as we climbed up the stairs of the institute.

'I am trying, Shona,' I said and made a face.

'If I am a distraction, I'll change my institute, because this way, it'll neither help your future nor mine.'

'No, no, please, it is not like that. I promise to pay more attention to studies. Don't say stuff like this.'

At school, all of us started preparing for the Teachers' Day celebration.

The rehearsals were so much fun that I never wanted them to end. I was gathering one beautiful memory after another.

Judgement Day

After a lot of practice and waiting, the much-anticipated day finally arrived. I woke up earlier than I used to because of the excitement in my head. I was expecting Anamika to wear the saree I had suggested. It was very important for me to look handsome to match Anamika's beauty, or at least be close to it.

Probably to embarrass me and to make my life disastrous, my sister had bought me a pair of smart grey trousers and a pink shirt. She forced me to wear it and assured me that I would look good. Imagine a tall, average-looking guy wearing the darkest shades and a pink shirt with buckets of sweat around his armpits. How would I look? What could have I done? I even considered skipping the whole thing and staying at home.

I spent over an hour in the bathroom that day, scrubbing my face. I completely ignored Vaibhavi's repetitive knocks on the door, urging me to come out as she needed to get ready for college. Nothing was more important to me than looking good. She even threatened to crumple my shirt, but her threat about not letting me borrow her phone for the day made me run out of the bathroom within seconds. She knew my weakness now.

I wore that pink shirt—the most horrible shade of pink one can imagine. What was even worse was that I had no matching shoes. I had been so busy that week that I had not even bothered to shave. I finally shaved today, sporting a small goatee.

'Vaibhavi?' I asked as she came out of the bathroom.

'Look, Aarav, I need to go to college. You have already wasted my time with your bathroom activities. Also, you're not getting my phone today. I'm going out with Vishal.'

'You're going on a date with Vishal?' I almost shouted, so that mom could hear it.

'Shut up, you . . .' she said.

'I'm the only one who knows about your relationship, so I was wondering if you could keep that in mind and lend me the phone today,' I smirked.

'Even I could blackmail you with your Pitampura hangouts, but I have something called humanity in me,' she spoke through her teeth and handed over her phone, adding, 'Only for today!'

'Till you and Vishal are together,' I laughed.

'We will always be! Once Mom's phone gets repaired, do whatever you want to. For now, please spare me,' she quipped and left.

Sometimes knowing other people's secrets helps you, especially when they are about people like my sister. I came to know about her relationship through the love letters that I had found while searching for my chemistry notes.

Vishal, her mate, was fair and of average height. He was an IITian. Vaibhavi wanted me to get inspired and become like him. He did not belong to our caste and that could pose a problem with my family. Well, at that moment, all I cared about was the phone. I changed the SIM and dressed quickly as Sunaina was coming to pick me up.

Sunaina was wearing a peacock-coloured saree. She was looking hot. Slim, fair, with straight black hair and blue eyeliner. Her fashion sense was perfect. 'We have to pick up Shanaya too,'

'What? But why? Pick Anamika up instead,' I said. She laughed.

Talking throughout, we reached Shanaya's place. It was rather a palace. As she came out, my jaw dropped. She looked spectacular.

A black saree with a deep-necked, backless blouse, and a pearl necklace. Her tattoo was visible too.

I couldn't help thinking about her in inappropriate ways. As she got inside the car, I was overwhelmed by her fragrance. I had to concentrate. Anamika . . . I kept mumbling her name.

'Hello, Sunaina, you're looking nice!' Shanaya exclaimed as they both started complimenting each other.

'Hey, Aarav!' Shanaya said and she placed her hand on my shoulder. The sensation was good, but it didn't feel magical like it did when Anamika touched me.

I shrugged her hand aside. We reached school within fifteen minutes.

I combed my hair carelessly with my fingers and adjusted my shirt. I looked around for Anamika. People passing by were staring at my shirt. Just then, I saw Anamika entering the school premises. I was rendered speechless once again and a voice in my head spoke, 'I love you, Anamika.'

I felt valued when I noticed that she was wearing the saree suggested by me. It was a maroon saree, worn in Bengali style. Her hair was flowing. She was in high heels, and coupled with the saree, was finding it difficult to walk smoothly. She had worn lenses today.

'Hi, Sunaina, you are looking good,' Anamika said, ignoring me.

Am I seriously looking that bad? I asked myself.

'You are also looking gorgeous,' Sunaina exclaimed and I nodded in agreement though no one noticed.

She surveyed me as I took in all of her beauty.

She raised her eyebrows.

'What happened?' I asked.

'You know what, there is a thing called courtesy. I don't know how someone could be so busy that his phone is always switched off. I had thought that we would come to school together, but perhaps you had other choices. I'm sick, am I not?' She spoke in a single breath.

I loved that too, the way she said it all, revealing how much she wanted to be with me.

She was upset and I didn't like it one bit. I stood there helplessly, thinking of what to do. She started looking around and tried to avoid my gaze.

As the day went on, students started showing up in glossy attire. Everyone was looking better than their usual selves. There were so many girls around me, each looking beautiful in their own way. My eyes were stuck on Anamika. They never left her. Every little desire for anyone else was being overpowered by a feeling more powerful than attraction; a feeling that I now truly recognized as love. I had made up my mind to propose to her.

The event had begun with some boring cultural programmes and speeches.

Anamika was busy with her duties as she was the coordinator. I wanted to catch her alone, but there were too many people around. And just when I thought I would get some private time with her, Aniket and Sunaina decided to spare each other and spend some time with us. Aniket was looking handsome, but Karan was a total faux pas. He was a bulky guy and perhaps to highlight his curves, he had worn tight trousers and a striped shirt that clung to his body. We laughed even harder when we saw Rahul and Oshit. They flaunted formal wear with brightly coloured sports shoes.

'So, what's the plan? Let us hang out at Saket,' Aniket offered. Anamika sat quietly on the window side, not responding to anything. I was concerned. I was blaming myself even though I didn't know the reason for her sorrow.

'So, who all are in for the plan?'

I waited for Anamika to raise her hands as everyone except her and I had already raised their hands.

'What about you both?' Karan inquired.

'Anamika!' Sunaina poked her.

'I can't come. I have something important to do. Sorry, guys,' Anamika said regretfully, still ignoring my presence. I felt my heart sinking.

'C'mon, Anamika. Get a life, you bookworms,' Aniket tried to convince her as I kept quiet.

Aniket was clever. He always managed to convince people to do things they didn't want to. However, it was not one of his best days. Anamika did not budge.

'So, you are automatically out too, then,' Karan scowled at me.

'Nothing like that, Karan, just not feeling well.' This statement had a purpose. Anamika finally looked at me and it was a look of concern. I winked at her and she tried hard to smile, but something restricted her. I almost choked. We really needed some time together.

When everyone left for Saket making faces, we both got some time together. This was the time I had been waiting for since morning.

'So?' I asked Anamika.

'So?' she echoed.

'I mean, where are we going?' I asked, anticipating a plan from her.

'Anywhere, I just want to clear things today. I'm feeling so blocked, Aarav,' she said as questions rushed through my little mind. Did she want a relationship? We decided to go for a walk to the nearest metro station. Both of us were silent for a long time. I couldn't bear my restlessness. Suddenly, her anklet fell. She looked least concerned about it. It was time for me to break the silence. Picking up the anklet, I said, 'What is the matter, Anamika? You look so upset.'

'Hmmm.' She looked lost. 'Let's go there. Keep that with you, I'll take it later.' She pointed to a bench beside the lake near Metro Walk.

'Look, Aarav, I want to share something with you.' At last she seemed to be in a mood to talk. 'Aarav, you don't know what I have been going through ever since I met you. It wasn't like this before we met. Things have changed for me. My priorities have changed, but at the same time, it is unacceptable for me and for everyone. I mean I think . . . you're just not . . . right for me. I'm not good enough for you!' I froze even as her eyes were filled with tears.

'What do you . . .' I raised my voice. She flinched. I tried to calm myself down.

'My brother loves a girl who is not Bengali. She is a Brahmin like you.'

'First of all, please calm down, and then tell me everything,' I said.

'My dad slapped my brother when he told us that he could not marry the girl they had chosen for him, since he has been in a relationship for the past three years in Chennai. Dad had a minor heart attack last night. I am so scared. I kept calling you, but you never responded.' She broke down into sobs.

'I'm so sorry, Anamika, actually my phone . . . I mean, the phone . . . I have one, but Mom doesn't give it to me often.'

She started sobbing uncontrollably and embraced me. I could feel her trembling as she held me.

'I'm so sorry,' I said, rubbing her back to console her.

'Is your dad okay now?'

She nodded and moved away from me. People were staring at us.

'So, what happened with brother?' I asked.

'Nothing. My brother had to follow Dad's decision. Otherwise, we would have lost Dad.'

'So, does this mean we don't have a future together?' I asked, almost speaking to myself.

'Aarav! Please, this will never lessen my love for you,' she cried.

'I'm falling madly in love with you every passing day, Anamika, and now you are saying that we cannot be in a relationship because your dad won't like it. Your parents should at least give us a chance, not now, maybe after a few more years. We cannot make such decisions right now. It isn't fair, Shona!' I paused to look at her reaction. She didn't respond, so I continued, 'I mean, if I'm not a Bengali, does that mean we aren't good enough for each other? This is so absurd, so suffocating. I can hardly believe we are having this conversation for real.'

'It's not about my brother, Aarav! It's about my dad's life. You know he came to Delhi from Kolkata thirty years ago with not even a single penny in his pocket. He got himself an education doing part-time jobs. He had to really struggle to give us the life we are living today. I'm not that rich, Aarav! We live in a rented flat. My brother has started earning only recently and he has shifted to Chennai. Soon, I will also be expected to shift there,' she blurted out, weeping. I looked away in silence.

'Please say something, Aarav. I wanted to tell you all this much earlier, but somehow the circumstances never allowed.'

I now told her everything that I felt about her and how special the moments spent with her had been.

'Look, I'm a simple guy. This is the first time I had started thinking differently, just because of you. Every moment we've spent together I have cherished. We would breeze through life just like we have breezed through the past few months.' I was trying hard to control my tears.

I took a deep breath and continued, 'I was waiting for a day when I could tell you everything. God reserved it for this day, but as soon as we got here, he changed the entire story.' My tears came pouring down. 'You must be wondering why I am telling you all this now. Please don't misunderstand me . . .' I sighed again and continued.

'Even if things don't work out between us, I want to tell you that whenever you need a friend, just remember that I am always there for you.' I was surprised at myself, the way words were flowing so effortlessly. I didn't know that I had such maturity.

'Anamika, come what may, I want to tell you that I . . .' I hesitated.

Suddenly, a hoarse male voice interrupted: 'Anamika!'

I turned around and saw a guy coming towards us. Anamika stood up when she saw him. She started shivering. I wondered what was going on.

'Kishnendu,' Anamika murmured.

'Hey, Anamika, what are you doing here? I was going to your place! Just came to shop a bit,' the guy spoke, putting an arm around her shoulder.

'Aarav! This is Kishnendu!' Anamika said, looking down.

We shook hands uncertainly.

'Kishu, he was just dropping me home. Our friends just left from here. We were t-too . . .' she stuttered.

'It's okay, dear. Now that I'm here, let's go. I've got my car,' Kishnendu said as he took her hand. I was purple with fury. All I could think of was punching him in the face. He was shorter than me and on the heavier side. But whoever he was, I had decided to dislike him. But who was he? Why was he behaving like that with Anamika? Why did she not stop him from holding her?

'You go, Kishu, *aami aaschi,*' she said. Kishnendu shrugged and walked away.

'Who is he?' I asked as soon as he was out of earshot.

'He is a family friend from Kolkata. He has come with his father to Delhi for . . .'

'For?' I questioned.

'For bhaiya's marriage.' She said and looked away. Before I could ask her why she treated him like he was someone who really mattered, he returned.

'Mr Aarav, Anamika has informed me how good a friend you are to her. But can I please disrupt your chat and take her with me?' He chuckled.

I absolutely loathed him by this time. All I wanted to do was to smash his pale teeth.

'I wish she could have stayed longer,' he continued. 'And Aarav, why am I getting the impression that you've fallen in love with her?' Another chuckle followed.

I reacted instantly. 'What is love? I don't know. But yes, I do wish from the bottom of my heart that Anamika never has tears in her eyes and that she always keeps smiling. If that is what you call love, then love it is.' I said, looking straight into his eyes.

Kishnendu eyed me intensely.

'It is better if you think of this as nothing. The truth is I'm nothing more than a friend to her.' I put it bluntly.

He raised his eyebrows.

'Goodbye. Let's go, Anamika!' I smiled at Anamika, but she seemed troubled. And then she left with him.

Just for a few moments, there had existed a story of our hearts. And then we went our own separate ways. It was almost like a dream.

I was stunned. I sat back on the bench and started weeping. I don't know for how long. I took out her anklet from my pocket and stared at it. It took me back to the days we had spent together, laughing, smiling, crying . . .

* * *

It was really dark by the time I realized that I had a place to go too—my home. I was going to be in a lot of trouble. I reached home and knocked.

Mom opened the door.

'Late again!' she shouted at me.

I just stepped in and looked down to avoid any eye contact with her. I had no strength left in me to explain my swollen red eyes.

'Wait!' Mom stopped me. 'Are you okay?' she inquired in the politest way possible.

I nodded.

'Hungry? Go and get some rest.' She patted my shoulder and caressed my hair.

I loved my mom dearly. She knew when it was appropriate to stay quiet and leave me alone. You share that kind of an understanding with your mother alone. Then I thought I should talk to Vaibhavi. I knocked at her door. She was probably studying.

'Wait, coming.' She opened the door.

'Oh, it's you. I thought it was Mom.' Once she took a proper look at me, she said, 'I guess you can come in and talk.'

I walked in and placed her phone on the study table.

Anamika's face flashed in front of my eyes and my heart became heavy. Tears rolled down my cheeks again.

'What happened?' Vaibhavi asked, placing her hand lightly on my shoulder.

My sister was annoying at times, but she was a wonderful person. She was warm and soothing now.

I knew her secrets, and so I felt like I could easily unburden mine on her. She stayed calm and heard my entire story.

'Sometimes there is not much you can do with such situations. You have to let things go. She cannot risk the life of her father for her selfish interests. god forbid if I am ever faced with such a situation, but I would always choose my family, no matter how much I love Vishal.' Vaibhavi tried to put things in perspective.

'But . . .' I was choking.

Was it so easy to forget things? Will it be so easy to move on? To see someone taking away my life, just because I am not Bengali? What does caste, ethnicity or religion have to do with the affairs of hearts?

I got back to my room and slept—an empty, dreamless sleep.

Dark Days

I woke up with a severe body ache. It must have to do with sleeping on the floor. My tears had dried out; now only pain remained, a pain so severe that it could kill me.

The whole day I stayed in my room, looking outside the window, constantly refusing anything that mom asked me to eat. Vaibhavi dropped in every now and then.

'Why don't you try to distract yourself by doing something that you like? Go out with friends,' she suggested.

'I feel too tired for any kind of activity,' I grimaced.

Vaibhavi offered me food and looked on helplessly.

Meanwhile, dad entered my room.

'You have coaching classes today, don't you?' he asked gruffly.

'I forgot about it. I guess I'll be late if I leave now, so maybe I can skip today?' I asked.

'Get up and change. I am dropping you. You won't be late,' dad said.

'Are you paying serious attention to your studies?' he asked on our way to the institute.

I simply nodded.

He patted my back. 'We expect a lot from you. Don't let us down. You won't, will you?' He looked at me with hopeful eyes.

I did not know how to respond.

Like always, I had no idea what was being taught at the institute. Anamika had skipped it that day. I wondered why, but I had no guts to call her and ask. I didn't even have the phone any more.

The day was unbearably long and the night was restless.

Why am I not a Bengali? Things would have been much simpler, much more wonderful. Anamika would have been mine and life would have been heavenly. These thoughts made me curse the society where caste and religion eclipsed the power of love.

The next day at school was harder than usual. My friends were busy whispering into each other's ears. I did not know the reason, neither did I try to find out. Sunaina approached me.

'Hi, Aarav!' she said in a hushed tone.

'Oh, hi!' I replied with a fake smile.

'Will you tell me one thing honestly?'

I looked at her, confused.

'Do you like her?' she didn't beat around the bush.

'What?' I said, baffled.

'Do you like her? We all know what's going on, okay. So please, tell me. Are you serious about her?'

I just looked down.

'I just want to tell you that I can see it in your eyes, what you have for . . .'

'Hi, Aaaaarav!' Shanaya interrupted the conversation. It was probably the first time I was thankful to her for interrupting a conversation. 'Hi,' I greeted and looked elsewhere.

'You seem pretty busy these days. No time for me. I mean, no time for friends, eh?' She taunted and pulled my cheek. I stepped back.

Sunaina eyed her indifferently and left me alone.

Our classmates started moving out for prayer.

'I guess we are getting late for the prayer, we must go,' I said.

'So, umm . . . how was I looking on Teachers' Day?'

Almost all the students were at the assembly. As I went to join them, Shanaya blocked my way.

'Don't you think it is rude to not reply when you are asked a question?' she asked and stopped me by placing her hand on my chest.

'Shanaya!' I said sternly and moved aside.

'Oh come on, Aarav, I just want to spend a little time with you.' She clutched my hand.

'We can do that after the prayer,' I evaded.

'Oh come on, Aarav, I know you like me. I have seen you checking me out. During that trip, you were too shy to ask me to sit with you.' She chuckled. 'You know what, you are just so cute. I really like you.'

She said and placed her hand on my cheek. I trembled.

'Stop shying away. Look, I am taking the initiative!' She gave me a seductive smile, but I was far too dejected to get seduced. I made another attempt to get away from her, but she caught my hand and placed it on her waist. I removed it.

'Oh come on, Aarav. You don't get chances like this daily, do you?' She once again placed my hand on her waist.

I was already in considerable discomfort; Shanaya was only adding to it with her crap. I pushed her away. Suddenly, A tearful Anamika appeared at the door.

'I . . . was just on duty. Sorry . . .' she said and left.

'Goddamn! Fortunately, she is not into gossip. I know she won't tell anyone.' I stood there frozen, as Shanaya hugged me from behind.

'Enough girl, move away!' I said firmly, pushing her away and leaving the class.

I needed to talk to Anamika immediately. That was the only thought in my mind. I needed to tell her that what she saw was not what had happened. She came towards me while she was checking for defaulters, but didn't even look into my eyes.

'I need to talk to you about that,' I spoke.

'You may go. No faults.' She walked away from me.

I had a strong urge to hug her, but perhaps I had no right any more.

* * *

At the institute, while the lecture was going on, I could see that Anamika's eyes were moist. I knew I had hurt her badly. Things were beyond my control.

I took my notebook and opened the last page. It had a few of our conversations and a few games of tic-tac-toe that we had played during the uninteresting chemistry periods. Back then we had been busy enriching our own chemistry.

'Please talk!' I wrote and showed it to her.

She gave it a glance and quickly looked the other way. She left as soon as the class got over. Her dad had come to fetch her. There was no way I could have talked to her.

'What's up, dude?' Aniket addressed me with a light punch on my shoulder the next morning.

'Nothing much,' I replied blankly as I looked for Anamika in the corridor.

'You're a lucky guy!' He began.

I laughed at the irony of his statement.

'Shanaya likes you, man! I mean, the world is after her and look who she has chosen! YOU, ass! You have done some real good deeds in your previous birth.' He laughed loudly.

'Will you just stop it? You know I am not interested in her. And this ends here!'

'Are you kidding me? You are not interested? Shanaya Taneja is the most desirable girl, and you are letting her go just like that? Don't tell me that you are so serious about the nerd girl that you want to miss this chance.'

'Aniket, I want you to shut your mouth.' I hated him then.

'Man, such an opportunity comes to very few people. Trust me, if I were you, I would not have given it a second thought. I would have left Sunaina and said yes to Shanaya.'

'Really?' Sunaina appeared from nowhere.

And that was how another love story ended. It happened because of one small conversation. I have no idea what happened next. I just know that his Facebook status changed from being in a relationship to being single. Anamika did not come to the institute after that day. My only hope was to meet her at school, but she would not give me a chance to talk to her.

School became dreadful without conversations with Anamika. Although I pretended I was okay, I was in deep pain and hoped that she realized it.

Another day, another disaster. Sunaina informed me that Anamika was going on leave because of her brother's marriage. I was tormented. I apparently deserved this for loving a girl who didn't belong to my caste.

I was fast tumbling downhill. I started getting irritated at the slightest provocation. My family was befuddled at my bouts of anger. My mood had become unpredictable and I would say nasty things to hurt people.

Then one day Vaibhavi came rushing to me with her phone. 'Here's a text from Anamika,' she said.

'What? Give me the phone,' I snatched it.

> You are cordially invited to the auspicious occasion of my brother's wedding on 23 November 2015 at City Park. Ceremonies begin at 7.00 p.m. Kindly grace the occasion.
>
> Regards
>
> Anamika Roy and family

Such a formal invitation! I wasn't sure if it had been sent by mistake or she had actually invited me, but I accepted it anyway. It was the only way I would be able to see her. Then maybe I could talk to her dad. There was a way to mend things. I was hopeful again.

First Kiss

The day of the wedding finally arrived. My heart refused to beat at its normal pace.

I had told mom to arrange for my slim-fit cotton suit. I wanted to look good. I looked inside dad's almirah and took out his expensive watch. Sunaina had been partially aware of the situation at Anamika's place. She had informed me that Anamika was leaving Delhi soon. The idea of Anamika leaving Delhi forever had frozen my blood. I thought how easy life would be if everything was like what they showed in the movies. I had also marked out that day to tell Anamika's parents about my love for their daughter.

'Hey, ready?' Karan called.

'Hmm, meet me in fifteen minutes. Near Vishwavidyalaya metro station!' I said.

'Are you ok?' he asked.

'Hmmm . . .' I said and disconnected the phone. I was frustrated and anxious. I left home without even informing mom. I was not in my senses. I was only thinking about meeting Anamika and her parents.

'Are you okay, man?' Karan asked as I entered his car. I ignored him.

'The girl's side must be rich, eh?' Karan said, breaking the silence.

'Why?' I said looking outside the window, observing the trees passing by.

'Man! Do you have any idea about the venue?' he exclaimed.

'Why?' I repeated, now in a frustrated tone.

'You are sick!' he declared. 'We are going to City Park, man! Imagine the ambience, the food and most importantly, the girls!'

'Great!' I said and went back to looking outside the window.

We reached the venue. It was big and lavish enough to hold high-profile marriages. Though Anamika belonged to a middle-class family, the girl's side had approved of her brother because he was an IITian. Moreover, he had agreed to live abroad with the girl.

As soon as we entered, Aniket greeted us. I had not yet forgiven him for what he had blurted about Anamika. I moved past him to get a glimpse of Anamika.

The wedding was taking place in typical Bengali fashion. Non-vegetarian food was all around, its smell overwhelming. I could overhear conversations of rich ladies.

'Nice girl, the groom's side is lucky to have her.'

'Yeah, the girl is highly educated. I've heard she works in some reputed MNC.'

'What's the use of such high education if she cannot feed her family?'

'What are you saying, Mrs Chaddha?'

'The girl doesn't know how to cook. What's a girl without cooking skills?'

'Oh, look who's here! Congratulations, Mrs Roy, wedding bells for your son finally,' a lady said cheerfully.

'Nice girl, eh? Belonging to a rich, sophisticated family, the only child of her parents. Mrs Roy, so what was your demand?'

'Oh, Mrs Chandra, we just loved the girl at the very first meeting. She's Bengali. Nothing else matters, not even dowry.'

'But who said it is dowry? The bride's side must have given some gifts to their daughter. As a token of blessing and love, you know.'

'Ummm, well, I need to go. Loads of work.'

She soon left the gossipmongers and they started all over again.

'Look, I told you, they aren't getting anything. They formally refused once for the sake of courtesy, and they lost it forever.'

My eyes sparkled when I saw Shona. She was draped in a cream saree, in typical Bengali style. She had minimal make-up on and yet she glittered. She didn't look happy, though. We hadn't talked to each other for over a month now. Then I noticed Kishnendu standing beside her. He looked funny in his off-white dhoti-kurta.

I went forward to greet her. She saw me coming and turned her face away. My heart broke, but I didn't lose hope. I wondered why she was acting this way. Why had she called me if she wanted to ignore my presence? Maybe it was revenge for the day she had seen me with Shanaya.

The wedding went on smoothly and Anamika kept herself occupied throughout. Karan and Aniket focused on the girls. I was biding my time to strike a conversation with her. I was constantly looking at her. She was busy greeting people—although she was grinning, I could see that it was not genuine.

After a while, all of us went to the garden where dinner had been arranged. A cool breeze was blowing.

'Hey, Aniket,' Anamika said as she came towards us. I looked away.

'I'm so sorry, I've been a bit occupied. I hope you guys are comfortable,' she said.

'And what about Sunaina and Shanaya?' she inquired.

'Oh! Umm, couldn't make it!' Aniket replied.

'But they have sent a bouquet and a very beautiful gift for the couple,' Karan said, rather formally.

'By the way, this is Kishnendu Banerjee, our family friend,' she introduced the nerd to them. Kishnendu was smiling broadly, while Anamika cut a picture in contrast. She was standing so close to me after such a long time, it almost took my breath away.

'Hey!' she said, smiling. I simply raised my eyebrows, trying very hard to smile.

'Hey, Aarav!' Kishnendu said.

'Do you both know each other?' Karan asked.

'Yes, we do! Very well,' I then excused myself to get some coffee.

After a while, I saw Kishnendu leave the group.

I went back, 'Hey, Aarav, take my car keys and please get the gift and bouquet here. We will leave after giving it to her brother,' Aniket requested as he grabbed some more dessert.

'But I need someone's help to carry it,' I said.

'I will come,' Anamika said and my heart skipped a beat.

'Yeah, that's great! Let me eat my dessert in peace. Delicious food by the way, this *mishti* too, Anamika.' Aniket winked at her. She smiled back.

She turned her gaze towards me. I looked into her eyes and they seemed to plead to me.

'Okay, let's go then,' I said and she smiled again. It seemed like a genuine smile. We left for the parking lot behind the garden.

We walked together, slower than ever. Walking together on the well-lit path strewn with flowers, both in our formals, I fantasized about my wedding day with her.

She was the one who broke the silence. 'How is your IIT preparation going?'

Wow! What a question, because obviously, this was what I was waiting to hear for a month now.

'Good!' I replied, suppressing my sarcastic tone.

The soothing music of shehnai played in the background. It faded as we went ahead.

We walked in silence, both of us stealing glances at each other.

I looked around for the car. It was dark everywhere. After a while, I spotted Karan's white i20.

I headed towards it and Anamika followed. The feeling that this meeting too was going to be in vain was depressing me limitlessly. I opened the car to take out the bouquet and the gift pack. At the same time, I removed my blazer and placed it in the back seat of the car. Despite the cold breeze, I felt warm and sweaty. All of a sudden, she broke the haunting silence.

'Please say something,' she said.

'What?' I replied as I turned back. I felt a lump in my throat as I looked into her eyes. This moment of sweet reunion was making my heart overflow. Her innocence was making me melt.

'Anything, just say anything,' she said, looking straight into my eyes, her voice cracking.

'I have nothing to say,' I sighed.

'Please, don't do this to me. You know it is not in my hands.' She was almost crying. Her voice was quivering.

I went closer to her and put my hand around her shoulders.

'Look, Anamika, the past one month has been the toughest month of my life. I had never expected or thought about the fact that you would abruptly leave me one day and I would have to live with our memories alone. It was something my heart refused to accept. That day when you saw Shanaya and me . . .'

'I have known Shanaya longer than you. You do not need to explain,' she interrupted.

She believed in me, trusted me blindly. This made my eyes well up.

I held her hand in my hands and looked straight into her eyes. 'I never ever thought I would fall in love. And I never thought things would happen so quickly and that we would be left separated by the tide of time and circumstances.' My voice broke.

'I love you, Anamika,' I said, my mind and body paralysed, this time expecting an answer.

She didn't utter a word, but pushed herself towards me. I was baffled. She hugged me slightly. She was shorter than me. Her face barely reached my neckline. She placed her ears on my chest. My heart was going crazy at this intimacy. She clutched my shirt tightly with one hand, while the other caressed my back. Then she grasped my hands and placed them on her bare waist. I was dumbfounded. She looked into my eyes and gave me the most wonderful smile I had ever got. I couldn't resist smiling. She stood up on her toes. Everything around me became irrelevant. I could not sense anything but her maddening presence.

She kissed my right cheek.

Then she touched my lips with hers faintly. She was breathing heavily. I could feel it on my skin.

I brushed my lips against her cheek. Then I claimed her lips. They were soft as rose petals. Her hands grabbed my neck for support, and I squeezed her waist. My hands reached for her breasts. We kissed until we had to come up for air. Our hormones were raging, and we swiftly moved to the back side of the car. She grasped me like she would never leave me. I kissed her nose, her lips, her neck, her forehead, her eyes, her ears, her cheeks, and everything that I could. She responded passionately. I rested my hands on her back, trying to unhook her chemise. Who says life would be better without hooks? Sometimes, pleasure lies in unhooking the hooks.

We were so lost in each other that we had completely forgotten about our plight. Suddenly, she pushed my hands away as we heard a baritone voice.

I didn't bother to look, but Shona pushed me away insistently, compelling me to look back. And trust me, I am glad I did.

Her dad was standing right behind us!

The moment was so unexpected and dreadful that for a few seconds, I was numb.

'*Ae, Anamika! What are you doing here? Hey, you, leave her alone!*' he shouted at the top of his voice. No one was around. He came towards us, his eyes had widened and become red. We were taken aback, petrified.

He grasped her hand and almost threw her away from me. Then he punched me. The ring on his finger had made a gash on my forehead. He slapped me innumerable times, shouting, 'What the hell were you doing to my daughter?" I tried to explain to him that it was all a misunderstanding. But he stopped me and threatened, 'I will kill you, bastard, you will pay!'

He was a heart patient in his late fifties, and this shock was not good for his health. He then fell down. He placed his hand on his chest and cried. His face twitched as he gasped for breath. Shona shouted and came towards us. Her father was getting another heart attack. Everything happened so quickly. Anamika started crying. Her father's eyes closed slowly and this scared me to death. Anamika clutched my collar and pleaded for help. I was so confused that my brain was just not responding to anything.

'Do something, Aarav. Help my dad!' Shona sobbed. She was panic-stricken.

'Wait! Just calm down, Shona. Please!' I exclaimed as I rubbed her shoulders to calm her down. Blood was trickling from my forehead.

I gathered some strength and lifted her father. I rested him in the back seat of the car and closed the door. Shona joined me in the front. I had never thought that the first time she would sit beside me in the front would be in such a situation. My life was full of horrible surprises. I was always in a state of shock because of one thing or the other.

I started the car. I was an amateur driver with no licence and the car wasn't mine either.

I drove as fast as possible. Shona kept crying, looking at her father again and again. She rubbed his feet frantically. Finally, we reached Max Hospital, not far from City Park. The security guard pointed the way to park the car, but I ignored him completely. I stopped the car on the side and ran towards the emergency ward calling for a stretcher, but the hospital staff told me to wait. I ran back to the car and, with the help of Shona, took him to the doctor's room. The doctor asked us to wait outside, while two nurses attended to Anamika's dad. All through, Shona was crying.

I stood silently, reeling from what had happened in the last one hour.

Heartaches

Eventually, I recovered from the numbness in my body and finally felt something. Terror, sorrow and panic took over me. Meanwhile, two nurses were consoling Anamika.

All of a sudden, a doctor came to me and asked, 'Is he your father?'

'Yes, what happened?' I replied as Shona looked at me.

'Please go and fill up the form and deposit the money required,' the doctor said and left.

'Sir,' I said as I stopped him, 'we came here in a state of emergency . . . money . . . umm . . .'

'Look, son, we won't be able to give him the appropriate treatment until you deposit the money. I can't help you with this, these are the hospital rules,' he said and left.

I felt helpless. I looked at Shona. She had calmed down a bit, but was still crying. Seeing her like this pained me immensely.

I thought of my next step. I didn't want to ruin her brother's marriage, but sooner or later, they would start searching for uncle and Shona. Then Shona's phone rang. It was her mother. 'Oh, Mom . . .' Shona cried.

I had to move fast. I told her, 'I am going, Shona. I will come back with the money. Please take care of yourself, act wisely. Please handle all this for a while. I know you will.'

My first objective was to arrange 5000 bucks for the registration. I had around 700 bucks on me. Then a brainwave hit me. My dad's Swarovski watch on my wrist!

I left the hospital and ran through the lanes of Pitampura. I was looking for a place to the sell the watch. Finally, I found one shop: Khanna Watches. I went inside as the shopkeeper was preparing to pull the shutter down. It was 10.30 p.m. Without wasting much time, I showed the watch to him. Without even looking at it clearly, he uttered, 'Swarovski metal, eh?'

'I want to sell it,' I said hurriedly.

'What? Are you sick? I don't have the money to buy such an expensive watch. This is a small repair shop,' he said.

'How much can you give me, Uncle?' I asked.

'See, you're going mad. Do you have any idea how much this watch is worth? Seventy-seven thousand rupees!'

I would be killed for this.

'Tell me how much you can give,' I asked.

'Have you stolen it?' He looked at my injured forehead with suspicion. I was speechless.

'Okay, I have 4500 rupees right now with me. Are you sure you want to sell it at that price?' He asked, still unable to believe that I wanted to sell it. It was the biggest deal of his life. It was the biggest deal of my life too.

'Sure!' I declared.

'Is there any problem, son?' he asked, wasting my time.

'Someone is fighting for his life and I am fighting for him. I need the money urgently.' He then quickly handed over the money. It was enough. I had Rs 5200 with me. I sprinted back through the dark lanes of Pitampura. My chest was aching when I reached the emergency ward.

Dibakar, Anamika's brother, was standing in his wedding outfit, holding the *topor* in his hand. Alongside him were Anamika's mother and Kishnendu. Dibakar came running towards me and slapped me. I felt helpless. The money slipped off my hands. A tear fell down my eye as I looked up at him.

'You asshole, what do you think of yourself? I will not spare you. The police will be here any moment. You're screwed, boy!' he said.

A few men encircled me as they waited for the cops. I wondered what case they would file against me.

'What about registration?' I gathered some strength and asked.

'Now don't try to escape from the situation. This will not help, Mr Aarav!' he said as he took out his phone and called someone.

He had probably taken care of the hospital formalities and the doctors were already at work. I wondered why Aniket and Karan had never called me. This was pretty weird, especially considering that Karan's car was with me.

Then I saw Karan and Aniket rushing towards us. But what I saw next shocked me. My parents and Vaibhavi were also with them.

'What is wrong with you? Look at him, he is bleeding,' my mom said as she touched my cheeks sympathetically.

'Mom, I just came here . . .' I tried to explain as Dibakar came over and started yelling at my father.

'Isn't this enough for you people? My dad is fighting for his life and you people are having a good time over here? Look, mister, your son is a bastard and when I tell you what he has done, it'll kill you if you have any self-respect.'

My dad was a sensible and kind man. He was mature enough to ignore Dibakar's rant, because he knew that the man was not in his senses, what with an ailing father and a truant sister.

'Lower your voice when you are talking to my dad,' I interrupted him. He grabbed my throat again. Aniket and Karan immediately came to my rescue.

'What if I don't?' he shouted at me and turned to my father. 'Your child has been using my sister for satisfying his sick desires. He is the reason that my dad is here, almost dead.' He was struggling to free himself from Aniket's and Karan's grip.

'This is a hospital! Move out and do whatever you have to,' the doctor came running.

'I will see you all later,' he said, pushing away Karan's hand.

'But, Dad, who informed you about all this?' I asked as Vaibhavi stared at her cellphone screen, probably texting her boyfriend. Mom was looking at the scattered notes on the floor as I made all possible attempts to avoid looking at her.

'Look, Aarav, it doesn't matter at this point of time. You should be here. Help them till his father gets well. Take my car!' Dad said as he handed over his car keys.

The support he gave helped monumentally. I felt a little relieved.

'Yeah! Lend him your car, your money, everything so that he can go and spoil innocent girls out there! Asshole!' Dibakar screamed and my hands automatically grabbed his neck. I smashed his nose. It felt like all my frustrations went off with that punch!

His nose started bleeding as dad tried to restrain me. Anamika and her mother came crying. They had seen me punching him, but they were not aware that he had provoked me. My mother grasped my hand in anxiety.

'You hit, dada! Aarav!' Anamika shrieked.

'He cannot say whatever he wants to, especially to my dad,' I said.

'Your dad? It's not your dad lying on a hospital bed and fighting for his life,' she cried.

'Shona, you are just . . .'

'Just leave for god's sake! We don't need your help any more!' She was categorical in her dismissal of me. I'd thought at least she would understand, but she was too upset to think rationally.

The situation became even more intense when the police arrived.

'This guy, officer!' Anamika's mother said, pointing at me.

'So you punched him? *Bohot garmi chaddhi hai kya*?' the cop asked.

'Sir, but he . . .' I tried to explain.

'Let's go to the police station and talk. Come along,' the cop commanded.

He noted down her mother's statements, while Shona cried even harder. It was turning into the worst day of my life!

My dad tried to dissuade the cop, but he would have none of it.

'Shona, just try and understand . . .' I wanted to explain the situation to her, but her mother pulled her away from me. Dibakar sat on the bench murmuring as a nurse treated his nose. I was also injured, but no one had treated me. Dad asked mom and Vaibhavi to go home, while both of us went along with the cop in his PCR. For the first time in his life, my dad had to sit in a police van. I felt ashamed of myself. My dad, a highly regarded person in his professional and personal life, had to live through these moments of shame because of his good-for-nothing son.

We finally reached the police station. 'Look, officer, let us settle this,' my dad said. I have no recollection of what happened next. All I remember is that I found myself home in a few hours. I do not know what my father did to make them release me, neither do I have any memory of my way back home.

There was blackness all around me and numbness spread across my entire body. I woke up after what seemed like days, a bandage on my head and a lot of pain in my chest. Mom sat beside me; she helped me get up. Getting up was painful. She looked at me with moist eyes and said, 'You have given us the worst experience of our lives. And we accepted and went through everything without a word. I don't want any more problems in our lives because of those fish-eaters. You better get that straight!'

I sat in my room, alone and hurt. I had no one to listen to me, to lend me a shoulder to cry on. I felt burdened. Guilt, shame and pain conquered me.

The pain of separation. The pain of having hurt the people I cared about. It was all beyond bearing.

Spaced Out

I saw no point in going to school. I had no guts to face Shona, that is, if she came.

I quit the institute despite all the objections of my family members. Time could not heal my wounds, everything was fresh. Most of my moments with her had made me smile but those last moments hurled me into hell. No one could help me, not even myself.

Karan and Sunaina visited occasionally to see how I was progressing.

Time passed, slowly, painfully. I did not fight the sadness. I let it engulf me completely.

Before I knew it, the board exams were around the corner. My friends motivated me to forget about everything else. They cracked lame jokes to make me laugh, but I just couldn't do it. Everything seemed empty without Shona by my side. 'Aarav, for how long do you think you'll rot in this room?' Karan asked in an irritated voice when I didn't respond to something he had asked me.

'I am trying.'

'I know how much you are trying. You seriously need to get up and start living. You can't ruin your career and your family.'

'You could not have said that so easily had you been in my situation,' I uttered rudely and turned my face away.

'He is trying to help you, Aarav, don't talk to him like that. Get up now and please try to study. We have an exam tomorrow,' Sunaina said politely.

Anamika's face flashed in front of me. Karan put his arms around my shoulder and hugged me.

'Calm down, we understand. We are here for you. We will be there, always.'

Karan started reading out from the physics textbook as I calmed down. He tried his best to make me concentrate, but I could hardly understand what he was reading. I was hearing but not listening. Soon, my friends left. All of us had our exam tomorrow and there was only so much they could help me with.

'Sunaina is on the phone. She wants to talk to you.' Mom handed me the phone as I was about to sleep.

'Aarav, you need to know this. I am sorry I have been hiding all of this from you for long.'

'What happened?' I panicked, suspecting it to be related to Anamika.

I was right. She began.

'Anamika's father got discharged from the hospital a week ago. Anamika was brutally beaten up by her father for reasons known better to you than me. There has been a lot of discussion in their family regarding her future. They feel their reputation in the city has been tainted by what their daughter did and the way her brother's marriage broke. So . . .' she paused.

'So? Speak up!' I shouted, unable to bear the long pause.

'Anamika is leaving Delhi in a few hours, for good,' Sunaina finally said and sighed.

'And you are telling me now? But where is she going? Chennai?' I shouted.

'I don't know about that, Aarav. She'd called me from a booth. She wanted me to inform you. She assured me that she'd call again and disconnected the phone.'

'Sunaina . . .' I said helplessly as my tears started flowing again. Mom snatched the phone, thinking that it was Anamika on the line.

'Stay away from my child,' she shouted at Sunaina and cut the call.

I got up in a daze. I had not even started to recover from the earlier tragic incidents, and here was one more.

She was going away forever.

I wanted to shout, but I couldn't. I wanted to see her once, just once before she left. I wasn't prepared to let her go like that, but there was nothing I could do. I had never felt so helpless.

I don't know how I managed to sleep that night, crying and longing for her. The next morning, mom pulled the blanket off me.

'Get up and prepare for your exams. We have had enough of this. Stop ruining your life!' she shouted at me. She showed no mercy that day.

I had no strength to argue.

I went to school with swollen eyes. Everyone stared at me. All of them knew about all that had happened with me. Rumours also abounded. I decided to ignore the looks.

I was in school after a long time. Sunaina and Karan came and hugged me. They were happy to see me, but I noticed that Aniket was missing.

I tried to force a smile, but I couldn't. I stood like a corpse in the assembly, with no expression or involvement. We walked back to our class. Two teachers stood in the corridor, talking. Anamika's name drew my attention to them.

'Yeah, she got her transfer certificate in a hurry. The situation must be critical,' Mrs Bahl said.

'Family situations can really make your life hellish. She was such a nice student. A scholar. I hope she gets all the success in her life,' Mrs Gupta said.

How could her parents spoil her studies? They are making her skip the senior secondary examinations. The situation had really gone out of control. During recess, I missed her passing by the window. I missed her echoing laughter, her sweet smile, the way she blushed when she saw me looking at her. I was going insane with every passing minute.

Days passed like that. My family had become very strict. They made me join the institute again. I went there, but lacked interest or concentration.

My pre-board scores had been humiliating. Mom and dad were constantly shouting at me. I felt that their affection for me depended completely on the number of hours I devoted to my studies.

Sunaina had received no further news from Anamika. I had no choice but to accept loneliness as my only companion.

Karan gave me Sunaina's example, telling me how wisely she had handled her break-up. He accepted that it was less intense and mild, but she had come out of it beautifully. As for Aniket, he was now seeing Shanaya. I heard stories of him drinking almost every day. I had neither the energy nor the will to care about him.

Eventually, as time passed, I got over the crying, but I was still very restless.

I had somehow taken the examinations and now everyone was busy with their JEE and PMT preparations.

I was left alone, all over again. Sunaina's father was getting a promotion and transfer from his office to Kolkata. She was also soon expected to leave Delhi, but she promised to be in touch.

Vaibhavi tried to sympathize with me. She told me that if I needed any help with my studies, her IITian boyfriend would provide it. But I refused, I assured her that I could do the preparations by myself.

I was finally able to suppress my depressing thoughts and focus on my studies. I could at least compensate a little bit for what my family had been through. This thought was the only driving factor towards my positive change.

Before I could realize it, IIT JEE was a few days away.

I was normal, but my father was extremely anxious. I had become a pessimist and was waiting intently for something bad to happen to me.

Out of the Blues

Sitting on the couch on a sunny morning, I was taking a break from my JEE preparations.

Then the landline phone started ringing. Mom would take care of it, I thought, and continued gazing at the fan. But I had to get up when no one picked up the phone.

'Hello.'

There was a lot of disturbance in the line. I even considered disconnecting.

'Hello.' It was a familiar female voice.

'Hello,' I repeated and tried hard to recognize the voice.

'Aarav? Sunaina here! How have you been?' she asked cheerfully.

I was really glad to hear her voice. Her call brought a smile to my face.

'I am fine. What's up with you? How's Kolkata?'

'Yup, it is really nice to be here. Really sweet people here. Guess what? I am trying to learn a little bit of Bengali from Ana . . .' she paused.

'From?' Hearing of Bengali reopened my wounds. However sweet the language was, for me, it would always have painful associations.

'From Anahita, a friend over here. How are your preparations for IIT going?' Her tone suddenly changed.

'Oh, it's going well. I am trying,' I responded in a low tone.

'Aarav, are you okay?' Suddenly her tone reflected deep concern.

'I am fine,' I lied. It came naturally now. It was better than explaining how I really was. Although I tried hard to suppress the urge of asking about Anamika, I failed. 'Have you heard from her?' my voice broke.

A few moments of silence passed.

'You still love her? What can you do to meet her?'

'I don't think I have the words to answer your question. I just want to see her. It's been so long. I just cannot tell you how restless I feel these days,' I said.

'She too wants to meet you for one last time, Aarav. Would you be able to do that?'

'What? What did you just say? She called you? Where is she? Is she fine? She said she wants to meet me? Tell me everything, Sunaina.' Tears started filling my eyes as hope bubbled inside me.

'Aarav, she and I are in the same city. She wants to meet you one last time. She cannot talk to you with her family hovering around her all the time,' Sunaina informed.

'She is in Kolkata? Is she fine?'

'Yes, she is fine. She really wants to meet you one last time. I told her it is not possible as you have your JEE this week. But . . .'

'When and where do I have to come to meet her?' I asked eagerly.

'You don't even care how far you'd have to travel? Your JEE? She was confident that you'd come, but I doubted it.

I'll mail you the address of my residence. Hold on a second.'

I waited patiently.

'Oh no, Dad has come. I'll contact you later.' And she hung up.

I checked and rechecked my mail every few minutes. I finally got Sunaina's address. She had mentioned one more thing—Karan was to accompany me.

I called Karan from my landline. We booked the tickets. It had been ages since I had met her. Her cheerful smile occupied my mind. I had not told anyone at home about it, but I needed to tell someone.

Vaibhavi would understand. I narrated the whole scenario to her. I had to deal with a lot of tantrums from her until she finally noticed the tears in my eyes.

Mom and dad were out for attending a reception. They came late and immediately went off to sleep.

I woke up at 4.00 a.m. I thought of bidding goodbye to Vaibhavi. I knocked softly on her door. She was awake. She pulled my hand and placed her phone in my hand along with 10,000 rupees that she had saved to buy a new phone for herself. She had tears in her eyes. I felt guilty. 'Please do take care of yourself. I'll say you're at Karan's place for JEE preparations, but come back as early as possible.' She said and pushed me out of her room.

I tip-toed my way out of the house and called Karan. We reached New Delhi railway station at 5.30 a.m. The train was at 7.30 a.m.

Sunaina's words about 'one last time' had started bothering me. The train whistled and left for Kolkata. Karan kept his eyes on me. He offered me several things to eat, some songs to listen, some things to have a look at, but I ignored each and everything. Stations came and went; not once did I step down from the train in the course of the entire sixteen-hour journey. I survived solely on water for the whole journey.

Karan was perhaps one of the very few who had enough patience to handle me. Any other person would have given up on me the way I was behaving. I was making things unpleasant and complicated for him as well.

We finally reached Howrah Junction. Obviously, no one had come to receive us. The air bore the smell of fish, and hawkers were selling *jhalmuri*.

We took a taxi from the station to the heart of the city. It didn't look like a rich city. It was rather congested for the likes of someone living in Delhi, but that did not stop it from being joyous.

Sunaina called Karan to tell him that her parents had left for some work. This was the perfect time to visit her.

'Kothaye jabe apni?' the driver asked in Bengali.

He wanted to know where we were headed to.

I had learnt a bit of Bengali from Anamika.

'Dada, Sreenath Colony jabo ami,' I replied as Karan looked at me in shock.

'What? I know Bengali!' I declared and looked outside.

I observed mud statuettes of Maa Durga on the streets. Preparations for the great annual puja had already begun.

Karan called Sunaina to inform her of our arrival.

I rolled my eyes as I saw Sunaina coming towards us, almost running. She hugged Karan and looked at me.

'Where is Anamika?' I inquired without even asking about her well-being. I was so impatient that I had forgotten all my manners.

'Just look at yourself, Aarav! You're not doing yourself a favour! Dark circles, skeletal body! What are you up to?' Sunaina scolded me.

'Tell me where?'

'She is reaching in a few minutes. Come, let us go to my house.'

'Is it safe to have guys at your place when no one is at home?' Karan asked.

'This is not Delhi, Karan,' Sunaina said in a matter-of-fact manner.

'Definitely safer than a parking lot,' Karan said and giggled.

'That's not a joke, Karan!' I protested.

Sunaina seated us in the living room and came back with tea.

'Have it,' she ordered. I picked up the cup to avoid any argument with her.

The doorbell rang, bringing my heart to a halt.

I got up before Sunaina and ran towards the door. I struggled with the lock, so it was Sunaina who opened the door. Anamika! In white kurta, and hair tied up. She had become skinny, but looked as beautiful as ever. Her brown eyes, already moist, looked into my eyes.

Tears flowed down our eyes as we surrendered ourselves to the moment. I stepped forward and took her in my arms. We hugged each other tightly.

'Aarav!' she said, in her sweetest voice. It felt amazing to hear her say my name after months.

'How have you been, Shona?' Sunaina intervened before I could ask anything. She guided both of us to her balcony and went back to the living room to join Karan.

'Shona, why? Why didn't you inform me before leaving? I know I have . . .'

She ignored my blabbering and said, 'Aarav, I love you!'

I fought the lump in my throat, but in vain. I couldn't utter a word as she looked at me with loving eyes. There was a long pause. We stood transfixed, looking at each other. I wanted to steal her away from there.

'Sunaina must have told you that this is the last time we are meeting,' she said solemnly.

'Last time? That has been taking the life out of me,' I expressed my deep dejection.

'Aarav, nothing can be done now.'

'What do you mean nothing can be done?'

'I'm helpless, Aarav. Dad has already fixed my marriage to Kishnendu, this week, on the ninth of April. I'm helpless,' she sobbed.

I froze.

'Things have changed and you know why. Nothing can be done now,' she said.

'Why now? You love me, I love you, what is the problem? We can talk to Uncle about this. I can't live without you, Shona. And Kishnendu? What the hell?' I muttered.

'I'm really very sorry. I don't have a lot of time to spend with you. I just called you here to tell you that I love you more than anything in this world. *Aami tumaake chhere thaakte parbo naa, Aarov, shottii,*' she blurted out.

'What?' I wondered what it was that she had just said.

My tears started flowing. It felt like a bad dream. She left within seconds as I stood there in disbelief.

I had come with a dream, hoping to turn things the right way, but life had planned something else for me. Nothing was left inside me. I had nothing to say, nothing to feel. It was like my soul had parted forever.

The Last Promise

'When are you coming back?' Vaibhavi's call shook me. 'I don't know, it will take time. Please manage things at home. Please!' I said as I pressed the disconnect button.

'Papa and Ma will be here in the next one hour. You need to leave. I am so sorry,' Sunaina said guiltily.

'Please tell us where we can stay. Some cheap motel or something. I am not carrying much cash,' Karan told Sunaina.

'Take a taxi from here to Bow Bazar. There is a little guest house there. Please tell me before you leave.'

Karan pulled me by my arm.

'Please take care of him,' Sunaina said as she bade us farewell at the taxi stand.

We struggled a lot. I mean, Karan struggled a lot, but finally found a lodge. It was like a small temple, basically a cheap-budget place.

Karan came to the room with two tattered blankets.

'You need tea?' he asked.

'Your phone is ringing, dude, attend the call.'

But then Karan took the phone from me and answered.

'Yes, Didi.'

'Karan whispered to me, 'Does she know the truth?'

I nodded.

Karan narrated the entire story to her.

'I will discuss it with him and let you know. Okay, all right, bye, Di.'

'So what's the scene now? What do you want?' he asked, looking straight at me.

'I am not going anywhere until she is married,' I said in a determined voice.

'But it isn't so easy, Aarav, I mean how can . . .'

'Sorry about this, Karan, but you are free to leave any time!' I said.

'Okay, okay. But we have to get back before your JEE,' he said as he shook my hands as a promise.

'We will. I just want to make sure that she is happy. That's it!'

He dialled a number.

'Dad, yeah, I am fine. Can you please do me a favour? Aarav's dad might call you today; tell him that Aarav is at our place for a few days for JEE preparation. Please, I will tell you everything once I come back.'

He turned back to me. 'Everything is settled at your place. Now we need some cash; I am coming back in a few minutes from the ATM.'

'Wait, I have around 9000 bucks.' I handed him the crushed notes I had kept in my bag.

I had never expected to go through so many travails at this age, but love makes you vulnerable.

* * *

Karan brought north Indian food from somewhere.

'Eat something for my sake, brother. I swear I won't take a single bite until you eat this.'

I sat there, looking at him.

'You must not take all this pain for me. I know what I'm doing is going to lead me nowhere, going to get me nothing. I will have another chance at IIT next year, but I will never get a chance to bring Shona back. I don't know if this is love or madness. I don't know what to call it. Whatever it is, it is holding me back. I just cannot leave without her, Karan. I can't,' I sobbed as Karan hugged me.

'Aarav, I can't see you like this. At least tell me what you plan to do,' he said.

'I don't know myself. I just don't know.' I cried my eyes out. We knew that our chances were not good.

He smiled and kissed me this time. And as I pushed him back, we finally giggled after a long time.

9 April, 5.00 a.m. I sat next to our luggage, observing the morning activities. It was her wedding today, and I was still sitting idly. Karan had proved to be a true friend in the last few days when I suffered so much of pain.

I still had things to tell her, things that I had never told her, but had always wanted to. I had often been unable to tell everything to her, but that day I felt like yelling everything out.

'We will meet Sunaina at 5.30 in the evening. You will be able to meet Anamika at around 6.00 when she will be in her bridal room, alone. Sunaina says that we should leave Kolkata today. You have already ruined her brother's marriage. And if something happens today, her dad will never be able to survive another heart attack. So tell me what your verdict is,' Karan said it all in one go.

'I think she is right, I should leave. I would, trust me. But I just want to meet her for the last time,' I said with a heavy heart. This was a nightmare, a never-ending nightmare.

I don't know when I fell asleep, but when I got up, it was time to go. 'Taxi!' Karan shouted, standing in the middle of the road.

The blue skyline was turning a deep orange. The Hooghly River looked more beautiful than ever.

'Shibpur, community farms,' he gave the address to the cab driver.

Soon, it got dark. The city roared at its usual pace, but my world was moving towards a pause as we whizzed past the various historical sites in Kolkata. I saw a dozen farms, but noticed that only a few had been lit up, while the others remained like me, buried in darkness.

'We have reached. Which farm?' the driver asked.

'I don't know!' I replied.

'Groom's or bride's name then?'

'Kishnendu,' Karan said.

'Okay!' he said and turned the taxi towards a small booth. 'Anamika weds Kishnendu,' he told one guy. I whimpered.

'Farm 18,' the guy at the booth replied.

I saw a big lawn, glittering with lights. A low shehnai music could be heard. A big hoarding displayed something I wish I had never seen—Kishnendu Weds Anamika.

We walked about 200 metres and reached the parking lot—another place that reminded me of some bittersweet moments. I saw a girl coming towards me, adjusting her saree. It was Sunaina.

'Aarav!' she exclaimed as she hugged me tightly.

'How is she?' I asked.

'Do you think she'll be fine without you? She is dying each day, she cries every night. She is doing exactly what you are doing to yourself, Aarav!' Sunaina was not able to control her tears.

'Where is she?' That's all I wanted to know.

'Come,' she said as Karan took my bags. We walked through bushes and reached the backside of the community farm. The bridal room was situated behind the main farm from where they would take Shona for the wedding ceremonies.

'Wait here!' Sunaina whispered as she made me stand behind the bushes. She went inside to check.

'All clear! Come,' she gestured.

I went inside. My heart was beating fast. I was shaking. Anamika sat near a huge dressing table, perfectly draped in a red saree with a traditional golden border. She turned and stood up, looking at me, not smiling. I forgot why I was there. I was so lost in her beauty.

She came closer, her hands stained with *alta*, a big red bindi along with tiny white bindis that decorated her forehead and her chin in a pattern. She wore a lot of floral ornaments all over her neck and hands that made her look all the more pretty. A shiny golden nose ring on her little nose added to her magnificence. Her eyes glittered as always, but this time with moisture. She came towards me. The tears had spoilt her kohl.

'Aarav!' she whispered. She finally smiled and hugged me tighter than she had ever hugged me. I was still, unable to react.

We both burst into tears.

I held her cheeks and wiped her tears off with my thumbs. I kissed her forehead trying not to spoil her make-up.

'Shona? Are you happy?' I asked, even though I knew the answer.

She looked at me accusingly. I kept holding her cheeks with my palms. Her hands were now on my chest. She banged her fists on my chest and then buried her face in it. Her bangles rattled.

'I am so sorry about everything, Aarav!' she said.

'Please, all this has happened because of me. I am responsible for everything. I ruined your brother's marriage, your father's health, everything. I am the only cause, Shona! I am sorry!' I cried.

'I don't know how I am going to do this. I am not ready for this at all!' she declared and cried her heart out.

'See, Shona, Sunaina suggested that I leave Kolkata now and let you live happily. So promise me that whatever happens, you'll be happy! Whatever you do, wherever you go, you'll do that with a smile. Promise me,' I said and lifted her chin lightly with my finger.

'Promise?'

'Live happily without you?' she looked stunned.

'Yes, without me, for me!' I said.

'Hmmm!' she said, pursing her lips. I thought she would fight with me over this, but she seemed too numb and disheartened. I was helpless and realized that I had to leave as soon as possible.

Sunaina came in without knocking.

'Aarav, you both don't have much time. I just called Dibakar dada, they are a few kilometres away from the farm,' she informed us.

'Hmm,' I said as I turned around to face Shona again. 'Shona, in life, all of us have an unspeakable secret, an irreversible regret, an unfulfilled promise, an irreplaceable loss, an unreachable dream and an unforgettable love . . . still, life is about being happy. Life doesn't stop, Shona, *life goes on*,' I exhorted.

'I have heard these lines somewhere else, Aarav!'

'Actually, Diego Marchi said that!' I said as we both chuckled, striking our foreheads together.

'Such a crook you're! You can steal anything,' she said.

'I'm not. I can't steal you!' I made a puppy face.

'I'm already yours, stupid!'

I sniffled and tried to fight back my tears. I started again.

'Okay, now listen to me carefully! There are lots of beautiful things around us. It's just a matter of how we see them and whether we're able to realize their beauty. In life, there are always some ups and downs. However, I believe that even in the most difficult situation, there's always a beautiful thing. As wise people say, everything happens for a reason. Life is indeed beautiful, Shona. Promise me that you will always live in contentment and will keep up your beautiful smile! I know how hard it is for you to bear all this, but I have accepted the truth, and I think you too should do the same.'

'Have you?' She did not believe it.

'Yes, I have,' I lied again.

'Aarav, it's hard to believe the truth. I can't believe it. I'm happy that you want to move on in life, and you should! I promise I will be happy in whatever I do and wherever I go, but can you promise me the same thing?'

She looked searchingly into my eyes. I was mute.

She slipped a paper into my pocket.

'You'll open this after you board the train. Don't worry, this isn't a love letter,' she said, looking away, biting her lips to resist the tears.

When the Heavens Cried . . .

I kissed her forehead again and left after a final look. She knew I didn't want to leave and I knew she didn't want to let me go. I choked inside, ready to explode. Life had put me through something that I was not ready to accept.

Karan and I left the place. We sat down on a wooden bench near Hooghly River at Santragachi Jheel, a few kilometres away.

I cried hard, covering my eyes with my palms. Thoughts of suicide came into my mind, followed by the crying faces of dad, mom and Vaibhavi. No, I could never do that to them.

'When is your train?' a low voice inquired. I ignored.

She shook my shoulders.

'Huh?' I said and turned back. It was Sunaina.

'Your train, Aarav?' she asked again.

'7.30 p.m.,' Karan said.

'It's already 7.00. I think you better leave. It'll take you half an hour to reach the station,' she said.

I picked up my bags as Karan called for a taxi.

'Howrah Station,' Karan instructed the driver as he kept our bags inside the taxi.

I waved at Sunaina. The taxi picked up speed and I realized that I was moving away from Anamika forever. Each and every moment I had spent with her was coming back to me. Karan sat still, not knowing what to do or how to help.

When we reached the station, I had a sudden and very severe headache. I sat on the bench. There was some time left before our train left. Karan brought tea for us. I sipped it slowly to cure that twinge in my head.

When we finally boarded the train and it started moving, I had this mad urge to get off the train and go back to Shona. But somehow I shoved it aside. I fell asleep . . .

Suddenly, I remembered Anamika's letter. I hurriedly took it out and started reading.

Aarav,

Maybe what I am doing today reflects lack of courage in me, but I cannot live with the truth.

Maybe when you read this letter, I would have reached where you always said I had descended from—the heavens.

I love you, Aarav, and I am glad I loved you till my last breath.

Take care.

Keep your promise, Aarav.

I am keeping mine. I am happy now, trust me. I am happy like never before.

Move on in life . . . we have had lovely moments together . . . the time we spent together was heavenly.

I am sorry for all that I have put you through. I love you, Aarav.

Do try to forget me and the memories we made together.

Anamika

I was in a state of panic and I started crying loudly. Karan woke up, alarmed. I shouted, breathing heavily. I banged my head on the corroded window.

I called Sunaina impulsively. Her phone rang, but no one picked it up. I tried again and again. I feared the worst.

'We need to get down!' I declared as Karan stared at me.

'What? Dude, you have your IIT exam tomorrow. Your father will be at our place in the next few hours to pick you up.'

'I need to go back . . . I . . .' I sobbed.

Karan took the letter from my hand and went through it hurriedly.

'Please don't cry, Aarav, she'll be okay. I'll inform Dad about this. You just calm down. Okay, we are going back.' Karan hugged me as I cried again.

'Nothing has happened to her. I know this is just a prank,' I said as I wiped my tears and laughed. 'I just want to scold her for this.'

Karan pulled the chain and the train came to a halt.

We stepped down from the train. Chaos reigned amongst the passengers. We were in the outskirts of Durgapur city. There was nothing around except for bushes, but we could see the city lights far away.

I sprinted towards the lights as Karan followed, dragging the luggage.

When we reached the city, it was deserted except for a few taxis, chaiwalas and drunk truck drivers. I breathed heavily as I knocked the window of a '24x7 Taxi Stand' office.

'Do you know the time? It's 11 p.m.!' a guy said with a yawn, waking up while removing his warm blanket.

'It's urgent, Uncle, I need a taxi.' I was about to cry again. But then I told myself that nothing had happened to Shona and she wrote that letter so that I'd come back. I was being really tough on Karan. My demands and expectations from him were getting impossible to fulfil with every passing event.

Karan tried to convince the guy.

'What happened? Anything serious?' the guy asked, concerned this time.

'Please take us to Shibpur trunk road, Kolkata,' I said.

'Please, Uncle, we are in trouble! It is serious,' Karan pleaded for his help.

'Okay! But it'll take around four hours to reach Shibpur and around 5000 bucks. Is it serious even now?'

We agreed. The uncle came out of his small office and lodged our luggage on the roof of the taxi.

I hugged Karan and cried out loud throughout the journey, moaning her name.

When we reached, it was almost sunrise in Kolkata. The skyline was slowly turning a deep orange. I hoped for a dawn in my life, but it seemed like my life had reached its end.

Shibpur farmhouse looked empty except for some labourers loading the chairs and tents inside the trucks.

'Is the wedding over?' I asked a guy cleaning the carpets.

'No wedding took place, baba!' he said, almost killing me with anxiety.

'Why?' I shouted at him.

'How would I know? We just came. But I heard that the bride fainted and they took her to City Hospital,' he informed us as I broke down again. This forced me to believe the letter. I walked back with paralysed legs. Karan hired another taxi and we headed towards City Hospital. I tried Sunaina's number for the thousandth time, but no one answered.

I rushed to the emergency ward as soon as I entered the hospital and inquired about Shona.

'Yes, a patient named Anamika Roy came here hours ago,' a nurse informed me, checking her records.

'She was in a state of unconsciousness when she was admitted, and, umm, it says here that she was reported dead. I am really sorry,' she said.

It felt like somebody had stabbed my heart. There was a whirlpool of pain, and then numbness descended all over my body. I fell down on the floor and cried harder than ever. I struggled to breathe. I couldn't feel anything.

Darkness replaced everything. I remember seeing Karan a few feet away, rushing to hold me. My eyes closed and every moment we had spent together flashed in front of me. I saw her laughing, crying, and hugging me.

Karan was talking to someone on the phone as I opened my eyes.

'I want to see her,' I demanded.

Karan remained quiet and called for a taxi.

'Manohar Das Road,' Karan said as we took the taxi.

'We are going to her place. Aarav, she is no more!' Karan declared. I had frozen, but my tears hadn't.

It had started raining.

Karan pulled me out of the cab. I was a corpse by the time we reached her residence. A few uncles stood outside the house with umbrellas in their hands, consoling each other. I saw some known faces. I was drenched, just like the day when she had left me after our first touch. Karan took me inside her house, clutching my elbow.

Shona! There she was, lying on the floor in her bridal attire, covered with a white cloth over half her body and a few florets sprinkled on her. She was encircled by a few ladies, including her mom and Sunaina, who were bawling. I was quiet now.

I went near her and no one stopped me. *Nightmare. This was just a nightmare*, I told myself.

Again, I was numb. But I gathered the courage to stretch my hand out to touch her. A spark went through my body. It hurt my chest. I looked at her lying down, with two cotton balls in her nose.

Her make-up was distorted. I fixed it. Her body was cold and pale. I placed my palm on her cheeks. I wished she would wake up the next second to yell at me like she always did. I buried my face on her dead shoulders and shook them hard. I still believed that she would wake up.

Suddenly, her mother pushed me away. 'Are you sick? Why have you come here? What do you want now?' she screamed.

'I . . . I . . . I . . .' I breathed heavily.

Sunaina tried to pull me away.

'Aarav!' Her father rushed forward with raised hand.

'Hit me! You want to hit me? You want to kill me as well? Do it! Do it now!' I shouted as I stood up. 'It was *you* who provoked Shona to death.'

'Please, Aarav, don't create a scene today at least. Let her rest in peace,' Sunaina cried, clutching my collar.

I heard Shona's father telling the relatives that she died because of renal congestion and asthma. It was all a lie. They knew that. He did not want the society to know the real reason.

Society—the reason why Anamika and I had not ended up together, the reason why she left Delhi, the reason behind the extreme pain she went through, the reason for her death.

I felt a burden on my chest. I fainted next to her body. I had no idea how long I had was down for, but the first thing I heard when I got up devastated me.

'They took her to the cremation place near Padara Ferry Ghat,' I heard someone say.

I got up and ran towards the main door. Karan stood there, waiting for me.

I looked at Karan with hopeful eyes.

He took me to the ghat in a taxi. The board said: Antimyatra Maidan, Padaraghat. A tall statue of Lord Shiva looked over the corpses.

There I saw Dibakar and Shona's dad. It was raining heavily.

Before they took her body to the cremation ground, the foot impressions of Shona were taken on a piece of paper. Her body was then kept on a pyre. Dibakar circled it seven times after the priest. Then he lit up the pyre to the repetitive chant of mantras.

As I headed towards them, Karan grasped my hand and said, 'Don't go there! Please! Please! It will create a scene. Don't spoil her cremation. Let her leave peacefully.'

I witnessed her cremation silently. Her face was still visible, lying on the log of woods. Tears rolled down my cheeks as Dibakar performed all the rituals. I could feel the pain of her body being set alight. I thought she would cry out any moment with pain. She had always been very sensitive.

After a while, everyone left, but I sat there till evening, looking at her burning pyre and sobbing. Every memory shared with her, her talk, her smile came rushing back to me. Her twinkling eyes, her hair flowing in the soft breeze, her saccharine voice, her small nose, sparkling skin and the sweetness she spread all over, was no more. It was all gone. I wished to see her smiling again, laughing at my lame jokes and clutching my fingers whenever I got upset. Her love, her care, her fragrance, I wanted all of them back. I wanted her back.

I lost consciousness again.

* * *

I could feel some people picking me up. I did not know where Karan was.

I suddenly realized that I was on a railway platform. I could hear the sound of an engine that grew louder. I assumed that it was the train approaching the platform.

I woke up screaming her name, 'Shona!'

I was in the train; my eyes were all teary and my whole body was covered with sweat. I was breathing heavily.

I hastily rifled through my pocket to find that letter Shona had given to me.

I sighed and started reading it. Her handwriting was so beautiful . . .

Aarav,

I have neither the words nor the time to tell you all that I want to.

I wished things went the right way, but destiny had other plans for you and me.

But here I am, making some serious confessions about my life.

2 July. I saw you for the first time. You sweetly looked at me from the corner of your eyes. Decent, my heart said. I told Prateek to go and check the other row for defaulters. I wanted to come close and talk to you. Sunaina noticed and teased me by saying that I had a crush on you, but the truth was much bigger. I cannot explain in words the way it felt when you opened my umbrella seeing me struggle with it. The rain, it was a good omen.

I liked your shy nature. I found it lovable. But I decided not to show that I was dying to talk to you.

I had heard somewhere that if you don't pay much heed to boys, they go mad and pursue you. But the greatest of theories fail on you, my love. You avoided me as well. I took it as a rejection. But it felt good seeing you not talking to any other girl.

Then came the trip. You were too dumb to ask me to sit with you, but I was really grateful to the wretched little kid, because he made us sit together. Little angel, wasn't he? The same day, Ma called me to say that Kishnendu was in town for a few months and they would fix our marriage if he brought it up. I couldn't handle it. Sunaina was busy with Aniket. As for Shanaya, I feared she'd make fun of it. I cried alone, but not for long. You finally decided to talk.

I thought of proposing to you, because I knew you'd never have the courage to do it, my shy love. I took you out for a walk with the same intention. The issue of my marriage stopped me. I was happy to have you at least as a friend. I didn't want you to expect much from me. I have also learnt the same from my life. Expectation is the mother of sorrow. I have grown up with crushed expectations and wishes. Now I have accepted it as a part of my life.

Coming back to my confessions, I was going so crazy about you, my heart refused to slow down when you were around, and my brain was always occupied with only one name–Aarav.

Cute little moments spent with you made me smile whenever I was in agony.

I was falling in love with you every passing minute.

We couldn't talk in school, so I joined your institution, risking your academics.

Oh! One thing just struck me! You know what? You are really bad at telling lies . . . I knew from the very first instant that you didn't have a phone.

Anyway, during the trip, I could see it in your eyes that you were falling head over heels for me. As for your proposal after getting drunk, it was hilarious, but also really special. You became unconscious, though I wish you had said some more words from your heart.

Coming back to the phone—when I had asked for your number, you had started making lame excuses, and had looked elsewhere. Liar! But I never wanted to embarrass you or make you feel guilty. Aniket had told me by mistake that it was your mum's number and I felt so special to know that you stole the phone just to talk to me. I found it really cute. I love you so much.

Teachers' Day was meant to be special. Everything was fine till the evening of 4 September, until dada revealed his relationship and Dad got disturbed. A fear grew in my heart . . . a fear of losing my dad. I somehow came for the Teachers' Day celebration, making an excuse at home that it could not be avoided as I was the coordinator.

Kishnendu had to visit us in the evening. He ruined my moments with you.

Things never went well after that.

Dada had to forcefully marry someone else. I was dying every day to talk to you. I was helpless. You understood my silence, no one else did. Your voice cured all the sorrow and fear in me. But we couldn't talk. I cried whenever I was alone.

Dad's heart attack on the day of dada's wedding took the life out of me. I died numerous times because of the guilt. I loved you and I loved my dad. You can't imagine how difficult it was for me to tell you to leave me alone at the hospital. My words said something that was completely in contrast to what my heart demanded. I wanted you, I needed you, Aarav.

The situation really went out of control. Dada slapped me for what I had done. He told me that it was my duty to set my family as my first priority, just like he had done. Some family friend joked about dada's jinxed marriage. Dad had to face sarcastic comments from many of his colleagues. He became agitated and finally, decided to move out of the city.

I protested. My studies were at stake. I wanted to be someone. I wanted to study a lot. I couldn't imagine myself ruining my life by marrying at this age.

But no one listened to me. No one heard me cry.

Dada repeatedly reminded me of my duties and responsibilities.

We moved out of the city. I couldn't contact you. It pinched me. I was not prepared to go without saying goodbye, but I had to.

The situations worsened after we came here. Dad's condition was not very good. Kishnendu's dad forced the marriage on us and reminded my dad about his numerous favours in the past. Dad had to agree.

I was glad to find Sunaina near me. I asked her to somehow arrange a meeting between us. I knew you wouldn't refuse. You'd come. When I saw you here, my firm decision of marrying Kishnendu faced a sharp blow.

And today, I am getting married to Kishnendu. I had thought about it a lot. I don't think I can do this, but at the same time, I can't risk Baba's life by refusing the marriage either. I can't run away with you, that's too impractical. But I can't love anyone the way I love you.

I love you, Aarav.

Move on in life . . . we have had lovely moments together . . . the time we spent together was heavenly. I am sorry for all that I have put you through.

Do try to forget me and move on in life.

Your Shona

A tear dropped with every word of that letter. I thanked god that it was a nightmare and that Shona was all right.

And I Moved On . . .

I don't exactly know what time we reached Delhi.

My eyes were all teary and there was fear in my heart. I had to take the JEE in a few hours. We took an auto from ISBT. As we passed Dilli Haat, I saw Shona and me standing there, laughing madly. I sniffled loudly, making the auto driver look at me curiously.

Somewhere inside my brain, I knew I had lost her, but deep inside my heart I could not accept it. I was in a muddled state.

I reached home. Karan's dad was seated on our sofa.

'Aarav!' my mom screamed and hugged me.

'Ma,' I said and started crying.

Dad gave me a disdainful look as he knew that even if I took the JEE today, there was no way I could crack it. Vaibhavi too looked unhappy. Mum and dad had lost trust in her because of me. I went inside my room to lie down. My head ached badly.

Mom came and offered me food. She had the ability to cheer me up no matter what. She was the one person I had unconditional love for—the kind of love that would never falter. The heart of a mother is a deep abyss at the bottom of which you will always find forgiveness and infinite love.

I skipped the JEE that day.

Dad and Vaibhavi didn't talk to me for days on end. It wasn't going to be easy to make them forgive me. Weeks passed and my attitude remained the same. I became silent. My eyes were bloodshot and my hair unkempt.

I used to stay up late at night and gaze at the fan. I would leave food uneaten, run for hours early in the morning. Karan tried to contact me, but I ignored everyone.

I finally got a phone for myself. Isn't life funny? When you have the access, you don't have the person. But I still called her number and left messages on her phone.

'Where are you, Shona? When can we meet up next? Why don't you pick up your phone? I miss you so much!' But no one ever replied. I still took my mom's phone to check if she had messaged me. I checked call logs to see if she had ever called, but I found nothing. I went through her old messages on Vaibhavi's phone for hours. I read them again and again, word by word.

* * *

One day, when I couldn't help myself, I went straight to Shona's house in Pitampura. I banged on her apartment's door. Nobody opened it, but I continued knocking it for half an hour straight, crying out Shona's name. I went to Dilli Haat and sat near the ticket counter waiting for her. I even tried to commit suicide.

It was at Rithala from a mall undergoing construction. I was at the top storey, looking down, wondering why I still existed. I walked towards the edge to jump. Suddenly, a hand pulled me.

'Are you sick? What the fuck were you trying to do?' It was Aniket.

'Aniket?' I said in a trance.

'Aarav! What has become of you? What are you doing here?' he asked.

'Come, come with me,' Aniket said. I went to his place.

'Sit!' he gestured and offered me a glass full of whisky. He forced me to drink it, and I gulped some of it down in reflex. I drank it in such haste that I puked most of it. Then I felt calm. I sipped on it again and looked at him absent-mindedly. The whisky was taking its toll on me.

'See, Aarav! I heard about Anamika. I know the whole story and, believe me, I was about to contact you, because I can't see you like this. I mean please don't do this to yourself. Life doesn't end. If something has to happen, it will. You can't let things ruin you. Do you get me?'

I nodded in response.

'So, what should I do?' I wonder how the words came out after so long and why I was trying to seek help from a person like him.

'Talk to Shanaya. She is dying for you, Aarav! She is feeling so low because of you,' Aniket revealed. 'She still likes you. We broke up in a week. She said she couldn't get over her feelings for you.'

'Shanaya, but I . . .' I struggled to speak.

I had tears as Aniket held my hand tightly.

'Maybe she can help you with all this; otherwise, I fear about your future, Aarav. Move on, dude!' He had cast his spell over me yet again.

The next day, I met Shanaya in CCD at Connaught Place.

'Aarav!' Shanaya said as she sat next to me resting her hand on my cheek. It felt good, though it was not like Shona's touch, but it was definitely something that would distract me.

'Shanaya . . . I'm sorry for what happened between us. I mean . . .' I said hesitantly. I wasn't sure why I was apologizing.

'Please, Aarav! Don't embarrass me. I mean it's okay, forget everything. Let's start afresh, and please smile now,' she said.

I smiled forcefully as she grasped my hand. She looked into my teary eyes.

'So, are you there?' she asked in anticipation.

I nodded in response, which she took as an approval.

I kept my promise and did everything to get over her. It wasn't easy, but we both tried together—Shanaya and I.

I was so influenced to move on that I was going away from Anamika a bit every day. Dad, mom, Vaibhavi and even Anamika had wished the same.

I knew it was against the dignity of my love, but I had to move on. I had to stop thinking with my heart. I started meeting Shanaya frequently. Anamika's memories, her words, her smile, everything started fading slowly. Everyone was happy at home with my changed behaviour. I started eating, drinking and talking normally, but I had lost my smile. I had the belief that it would come back one day and I was waiting for that day to come. I believe that losing someone will lead you to two paths: either you will never fall for anyone again or you will fall for everyone to get over your loss. I had been convinced to walk on the second path.

Shanaya started demanding physical intimacy—almost always. Gradually, I relented, thinking that this too was love.

I stepped outside the train. It was hazy all around. I could not see anything properly; there was a lot of mist. I looked all around. I saw nothing but an empty railway platform. Suddenly, my train whistled to leave. I turned around as I saw Anamika coming towards me out of that fog in the same attire she wore that day. She looked beautiful. Her hair blew in the breeze. She didn't look bothered about her marriage or anything else. She smiled and placed her hand on my cheek. It felt like I was in heaven for a few seconds.

'Shona,' I screamed.

'Aarav! See, I am happy now. Are you happy?' she asked softly.

'Yes, I am. I always wanted this, just your happiness. No matter how or with whom . . .' I asserted.

'Leave that and listen! Now I want something from you,' she said in her childish manner. I nodded in agreement and, for the first time in months, I smiled. The haze was not gone yet. I looked into her eyes as she said, 'Aarav, I love you. I love you like no other thing in this world. You might not know how much that is, but I could never have been able to get through this without you. I had silly thoughts, but your smile always stopped me from doing anything harmful. Let me not waste much time, but promise me one thing before you leave. You'll never break down and you will always be happy at every stage of your life! I have to leave now. Someone's calling me, and yes, all the best for your life. I LOVE YOU!'

It grew hazier and she got lost somewhere in that smog. I sprinted after her, but she had left me, yet again.

The alarm clock woke me up and I had her anklet in my hand—from that meeting.

Everyone was finally happy with me, but I was not happy with myself. I scribbled something on a piece of paper that morning. It was the same paper on which she had written her phone number for me.

Guzarta hun aaj bhi jab un galiyon se main,
To waqt kahin ruk sa jata hai,
Dil karta hai kuch masoom sawaal,
Par naa dhadkano se koi jawaab aata hai,
Rukk si jaati hai ye dhadkane bhi waqt ke saath,
Jab jab un lamho ka khayal aata hai.

Dekhta hun aaj bhi main jab unhe vahi apne saath,
Vo nazara hothon par hassi aur aankhon mein chand aansu bhar lata hai
Fir bhi un ashko ki bheed mein ik aansu esa chalak aata hai,
Jinme un yaadon ka gehra aks nazar aata hai,
Dhoondta hai dil unhe, jinke hone se dhoop me bhi hoti thi chaaon,
Intezaar hai to bas itna ke zindagi me vo lamha fir kab lautkar ata hai . . .

Epilogue

I had moved on in life, but I had not been able to move on from her memories in my heart.

'This is how I became what I am today,' I said as I looked around at everyone.

Radhika's eyes were full of tears and Mishka was sniffling too. Karan and Deb managed to control themselves, while Devika was almost asleep, but her eyes too were moist. Too much alcohol!

'So, how did you move on then? I mean, what next?' Mishka asked in a low voice.

'Shanaya you mean?' I asked. As Deb came and sat next to me, placing his hand on my shoulders.

'Yes!' she said.

'Ahh! We broke up in two months. She got what she wanted. Actually, she left for Europe to pursue her studies. That was not love really. She told me that she was leaving me. It all finished in a fraction of time,' I said.

'Then?' Deb asked this time.

'Then? Nothing. I went on with college, had a few relationships. I became so selfish that I ruined lives to keep myself happy. I wanted to be occupied, so I fell into relationships that lasted just months, weeks, days, and even hours at times. It sounds strange, but I did that because I was made to do it. I chose this path unwillingly, but kept walking on it willingly. It might be because it helped me to some extent. I cannot say that I have forgotten Anamika. To be frank, my love for her has grown since the day she left me. There can be a number of reasons why people leave you, but what they leave inside you is something that can never be forgotten. It becomes a part of you, no matter how much time has passed since their departure from your life,' I said, fighting tears.

'Where is Anamika now?' finally Radhika asked.

'Well, I never talked to anyone about her after all that. So I don't exactly know her whereabouts, but I hope she's happy wherever she is now,' I smiled.

Radhika stood up, came towards me and smiled. She hugged me tightly and said, 'Sorry!'

'I'm sorry, Radhika. You don't have to be!' I said and smiled at her.

'You're so good, Aarav, please don't spoil yourself,' she said

'I will!' I winked.

I hugged Karan. He was the one who stood by me through thick and thin. He had a cure for all my pains.

'You know everything, so why are you still awake?' I asked Karan.

'To witness the purest form of love in your eyes!' he said and patted my shoulder.

'I'm sorry, Aarav, I always misunderstood you!' Deb said.

'You understood me correctly, Deb. The only thing is that it was not the real me!' I smiled.

Deb, Karan and Radhika left, carrying Devika inside the farmhouse, as she sobbed dreamily.

An unusual night had come to a valuable end. I looked at my watch; it was 6.00 a.m. The sun had risen with an orange glow. The first morning of the year had begun well.

The breeze was blowing the bonfire ash. Birds were chirping, empty vodka bottles were lying in indolence and the grass was wet. It was a typical 1 January, but it felt special.

'Don't you think any father would have behaved the same way if he had caught his daughter like that?' Mishka ended the silence abruptly.

'I think yes. In fact, I feel I was wrong in getting carried away in the moment. I mean, I don't object to any such deeds in a relationship, but we should have thought about the situation around us. It was the goddamn parking lot of the banquet of her brother's marriage,' I answered, frustrated with myself.

'Hmm, maybe. But her father kept the society as his priority, completely neglecting his daughter and her needs. He could have tried to be more accepting. That way, he could have at least reduced the intensity of the suffering brought to you both and their family as well,' Mishka added.

A thought struck me.

'I want to write about this, Mishka,' I said, taking a deep breath.

'What? Write what exactly?' she asked, bending towards me.

' About all that happened last night,' I smiled.

'Are you nuts? What was so special about last night that you want to write about it?' She was not convinced.

'I mean what I realized last night.'

'Elaborate? How do I know about your realizations? I need more context,' she said.

I continued, 'I mean, my first love left me heartbroken. I got out of it believing that love is terrible and it can only make you suffer. I focused only on the dark side of the story. Did I ever try to feel the love around me? No, I didn't. I indulged in the worst of accomplishments; peer pressure might have been one of the reasons. But I accepted and followed it blindly. I never gave my life a chance. I never learnt from it.'

Mishka gave me a quizzical look.

I continued, 'But that is not what love is all about. Love not only brought me pain and swollen eyes, it gave me moments to cherish for a lifetime. I took the bad experiences like a coward. I didn't come out of it. I didn't forgive my life. I didn't let it go. Things could have been better. I could have made them better; no one else could have. Love is not an easy affair, but it undoubtedly is the most beautiful feeling in the world.'

'Ahaann, love guru!' Mishka winked at me.

'It is not just about love. In any aspect of our life, we do the same. Don't you think? One bad experience and we restrict ourselves from trying again. We don't try, we don't live. We imprison the spontaneity of our life. We fear the thing that brought us disappointment.'

'My god! You are full of philosophical shit! But this sounds like a universal truth.' She looked at me gravely.

'Yeah, I might become a baba someday.' I unfolded the collar of my shirt.

Mishka threw a stone at me playfully.

'But seriously, man, I agree. We do forget that life has its own ways of teaching us its lessons. I hope that your story inspires people to take life positively and a bit less seriously. Bad moments and good ones are part and parcel of life. That's how life goes on.'

'Ahaann, I am contagious,' I said as we high-fived. 'So when are we meeting next?'

'Whenever you want!' she said.

'*Akhon thekei shuru kori, bokaa*!' I said and winked at her.

'What?' she stared at me wide-eyed and we both chuckled.

# Acknowledgements

Life seems to be a vicious circle of uncertainties. I have always been uncertain: from the day this book was released to the day it became a national bestseller. But there are a few reasons and a few people who make life beautiful amidst all these uncertainties. They are the sole motivation and inspiration behind everything big I have done. They actually make me forget all the outcomes and encourage me to go on and make it as best as I can.

My first thanks to the Almighty, my Guru, and my parents for all the selfless support, care, and love.

My sisters, Vidhi and Purti, for being so hopeless about me every time! They're the best sisters in the world.

People come and go, but each one of them leaves an impression on your life—some good, some bad. I would like to thank all those who have helped me knowingly or unknowingly.

Mohnish Rajput, for being whatever he is. Sahil Narula, my twin brother. Gitanjali Babbar, for her beautiful stories, and the way she narrates them (with a clap and a huge smile). My Zohanian gang and Xavier's group, for the wonderful moments we spent together.

Ayush Dinker and Sunill Kaushik, for making people judge the book by its cover. Thank you for such amazing covers. Aditya Kapil, for his time to make a fantastic teaser video.

Last but definitely not the least, Gunjan Narang, for being there.

Anurag Garg

Ma, Papa, even if I have not voiced it, I am thankful to you for being the patient and understanding parents that both of you have been. I am a proud daughter.

Shreyanjana, my love, thank you for reading this book and providing honest feedback, and for keeping it in the front row of your treasure house of books. I simply adore you.

Nikita, many hugs for your open-heartedness and for bearing with every word of this book. I am glad I could receive your critical reviews at last.

Nitti, immense love for your encouragement, love and (not-so-long) stress-busting drives.

Richa, I cannot thank you enough for reading the book carefully to look for pages that made people cry. Yes, you can kill me with a hug.

Ayush Dinker and Sunill Kaushik, I applaud your creative efforts for making the covers that have given the book its identity until today.

Anurag, for your eternal patience with me before and after the book came into being. Thank you for being a friend before being a co-author.

Team Srishti, for embracing us novices and giving us the right opportunity at the right time.

Random House, for hand-holding us and helping us to achieve the current look and form of the book.

You, the reader holding this book now, my heartfelt gratitude for reading our work and taking out the time to write to us. We owe the success of the book to you.

Gunjan Narang